THE
SHAMAN'S SECRET

The shaman went straight to the space between the contestants and seated himself cross-legged on the floor. Chael saw Lissa raise one perfect eyebrow. She obviously didn't know the shaman's secret.

"Lissa," Chael cried, "it's a mirror." But he was pulled away before he could say more. Lissa deliberately turned her back on him. Helplessly, he watched as the contest began. The shaman's silver headdress seemed to cloud, and the room grew misty. Chael watched incredulously as Lissa's form flowed and changed. She grew taller, to half again her own height. Her bones were long, her skin taut. Silver claws tipped her fingers. She wore a necklace of human skulls, and each skull winked with diamond eyes. Smoky wraiths whirled around her. Her lips were red with fresh blood, and her face twisted into a smile that made him shudder. . . .

THE
OZINE
CONQUEST

C.M. Gilbert

LEISURE BOOKS   NEW YORK CITY

A LEISURE BOOK

Published by

Nordon Publications, Inc.
Two Park Avenue
New York, N.Y. 10016

It was the time of the great frontier, when humanity expanded chaotically through the Galaxy. Among many, it fostered a bold and reckless search for freedom. One such was Chael, soldier of the Fenmark, Chael the stranger, Chael the hero, Chael the one-armed . . . .

The Ozine Chronicles

1

The moon shone full in a cloudless sky as Chael pulled
the black hood over his head and climbed silently down
the wall of the barracks. It was early spring, the kind
of night that brought the Coss down out of the moun-
tains. He longed to be back on the border where he'd
spent most of his life guarding the Fen from Coss
raiders, but now he was Chael the hero, a one-armed
man, fit only for watching the governor's clerks. He
spat in disgust. What did it matter that his left hand
was metal when it was stronger than any hand of flesh
and bone?

Quietly, he slipped past a lighted window. There
was laughter inside, but he was in no mood for com-
panionship. He smelled ozone from the recently-ended
rain and, over that, the sharp smell of the sea. He
climbed silently, not wanting to arouse the guard. The
grass around the governor's building was short and
stiffly formal. The woods beyond were wild. He had
to cross the governor's forest to get to the beach.
Halfway across the lawns, the crunch of gravel alerted

him, and he skulked behind a flowering shrub as a pair of patrolling guards marched by.

The woods were dark, and the wind made a rushing noise in the branches. The scent of the trees was sharp and crisp. He walked slowly, savoring the night. At length, he came to the cliff above the beach.

It was a small beach, seldom used, reachable only by a difficult climb down the steep cliff face. Twenty meters below lay a long, flat stretch of sand and driftwood. The tide was going out. The sand was smooth and hard, and the seaweed smelled of iodine. Chael stripped, ignoring the chill and the small, sharp stones poking his bare feet. He ran into the water and gasped for breath in the icy cold. He swam ferociously until he was warm and exhausted.

Slowly, he swam back to the beach, straining against the tide. Back on the shore, he toweled himself on his tunic and dressed slowly. He felt relaxed at last, almost drowsy. Running an office full of clerks didn't give him the exercise he was used to. He wondered if he'd grow fat like Hopper and puff when he walked. He snorted, better to just keep swimming out to sea some night, but that was too much like giving up, and he was too stubborn for that. His stubborn pride had cost him his hand in the first place. The Coss fire torture hadn't made him reveal where his company's weapons cache lay hidden. He'd escaped from the Coss camp and come back a hero—and a cripple. His left hand was metal, so they gave him a nurse's job.

His black thoughts were interrupted by a glow of light. It wasn't the moon—which now hung low on the horizon—but a small, bright pinpoint. A humming emanated from it, like the drone of dynamos. The power seemed out of all proportion to the size of the light. The hairs stood up on Chael's bare arms. He watched narrowly. The light grew into a silver oval,

8

rapidly spreading to nearly two meters tall and a meter wide. Chael walked around the shimmering oval. Except for the silvery light it emitted, it was too thin to be seen from the side. The back looked the same as the front. Chael regarded it thoughtfully, remembering old stories his mother had told him.

He was about to touch it when he heard the distant shouting. Hissing noises followed. A blaster bolt shot out of the oval and seared the driftwood log where he'd been sitting. Chael jumped back, crouching. He didn't have a blaster with him, but he carried a serviceable knife. He held it ready in his hand. Suddenly, a fleeing figure ran out of the oval. A line of blaster fire seared the runner. There was one short scream and the thud of the body falling on packed sand. The oval faded, disappearing much faster than it had come.

Chael knelt to examine the stranger. No one else had heard the scream. He'd been tall, slender, and blond. It was impossible to tell more. The body was blackened cinders from eyes to knees. Chael sat back on his heels. The first bolt had done the job. The rest were unnecessary. Malice or fear? he wondered.

The stranger wore a grey overall. It told him nothing. No doubt a full investigation by the proper authorities would reveal more, but he had no mind for any more entanglements with the bureaucracy. Near the stranger's outflung hand lay a slender, white wand. Eyes widening, Chael picked it up. So the stories were true. His mother had simply reported fact. He held an Ozine wand, product of a science so advanced as to make its artifacts seem like magic to other races.

He used a stick to dig the stranger's grave. A small, circular hole in the damp sand close to the base of the cliff made a snug resting place. He laid leaves in the grave and placed more leaves over the body, then filled the hole with sand and covered it with rocks. Chael

9

recited the simple soldier's prayer he'd said so many times before over other graves, and the task was done. The wand he slipped into the pocket of his tunic. He had other plans for it.

All the next day the Ozine wand occupied his mind. The clerks bent over their terminals as usual, but he didn't notice. Chael racked his memory for scraps of long ago conversations. He'd never expected to grow up planetbound. He was the child of Rim Runners; the ship was his home. His parents had carried lightweight, high-value cargo from the settled inner worlds to the pioneers on the edge of human space.

Many strange tales were told there, and the story of the Ozine wands was one of the strangest, the more so because it was true. The wands had been fashioned for some ancient prince, three of them. And they opened the door to anywhere—if one knew how to use them. That was the hitch. No one knew now with certainty except perhaps the Ozine, if that fabulous race still existed. Still, he held a fortune in his pocket.

He frowned at the clerk who held out yet another document. Without bothering to read it, he pressed his thumb to the seal, and the clerk hurried away. He settled back in his chair, hands behind his neck. If he tried to sell the wand, the red tape would be interminable, and some enterprising thief would very likely slit his throat and take the wand before he had time to claim his prize. But he could use it himself.

It was dangerous, but he was used to danger. He'd given ten years to Fenmark, from the time he'd entered the academy as an orphan stranger of eleven standard years until today. He'd served the Fen of Fenmark to the best of his ability. Now, there was no place for him. He longed for a ship. If he could only make it to the Rim, to the frontier, he'd have a chance to be truly free.

Sunset found Chael in the woods again. Tonight, he wore a jacket over his tunic, and he carried a blaster. An emergency pack was strapped on his back. He unholstered the blaster, holding it in his right hand of flesh and blood. His metal hand held the wand. He pressed the stud and waited for the silver oval to appear. He didn't know where he was going or what he was getting into. He might be dead meat in another moment—or he might be free. The power of the oval throbbed around him. The hairs rose on his scalp. He listened carefully, but there was no sound of voices or blaster fire. He took three running steps forward and dove through.

He fell forever through silver. He didn't breathe. His heart was silent. Effortlessly, his body continued its timeless fall. Then eternity ended, the silver thinned, and he was moving again. He picked up speed, rolling in a forward dive designed to carry him past any waiting guards before they had a chance to aim and fire. He gripped the blaster tightly, ready to return fire if need be. He rolled, landing against a wall and spun into a crouch. No beams sizzled around his ears. No alarm sounded. He appeared to be alone. But this was where the stranger had come from. The walls were scarred by sooty black scorch marks where the rock itself had burned.

He was in a tunnel. The walls ran on into infinity, the strips of lights running along the top converging on some distant point. It was dusty, and there were scruff marks in the grit on the floor. The band of light was scored in places and dark in others. The corridor seemed abandoned. There were no windows, just an unbroken line of ivory wall. Behind him, the way ended in bare rock that still showed the marks of some excavating tool.

There was only one way to go. Cautiously, he started down the corridor. There were no cross-tunnels, only dust and scorch marks bearing mute witness to the destruction that had passed through so shortly before. The tunnel seemed to go on forever. But the breeze was fresh, despite the dust. He wasn't worried, only cautious and curious. He wanted to know more, but he didn't want to run unwarned into whoever had blasted the stranger. There was an open space ahead, a widening of the way. A piece of abandoned machinery almost filled it. By the cutting lasers on the front, it was probably the excavator that had carved the tunnel.

Chael stopped to examine it, running his hand over the dusty, long-unused surface. The far side seemed the same until he spotted the glove. It was out of place. The glove was clean, for one thing, and made of a supple grey material.

Chael put it in his pocket and sat on the platform of the excavator. He pulled one of the ration bars from the emergency kit and drank a swallow of water. He put the cap back on the canteen and shook it. Enough for another day, he judged.

Munching the tasteless ration bar, he considered the tunnel; it appeared deserted, but someone had been here not long ago. His metal hand closed around the wand in his pocket. He still had a way out. He let go of the wand and drew out the hand. Clenching and unclenching it, he admired the play of metal cables under the clear plastic. He could have had it colored to match his remaining hand. In fact, the medics had urged him to do so. But Chael refused, taking perverse pleasure in the shock and discomfort his disfigurement aroused in the governor's palace. His mother would have disapproved, and his father would have laughed. But they were both dead, caught by Coss raiders who'd ranged unexpectedly deep into the interior, so what did it matter? The ship had been sold to pay for his upbringing, and he'd made the Coss pay in turn.

But he was always the outlander, the stranger. Oh, his dark hair and olive skin blended well enough, even though he was a little too tall and too thin, but his eyes marked him. No Fen of the Fenmark had blue eyes.

He traveled for some time down the corridor before he heard the soft, high surf-sound of many voices. Ahead, there was a brighter light. Chael slowed as he approached it. The corridor came to an abrupt end. Hugging the wall, he peered out into the cavern. It stretched into the mist and above to the dome of heaven, or so it seemed to Chael. A vast, crystal roof separated the cavern from the stars. They shone hard and clear, without any of the wavery twinkle of atmosphere between them and him.

There were people too. They looked like children. Of medium height and very slender, they wore pastel robes that fell in folds from shoulder to ankle, leaving their thin arms bare. Their voices were soft. Chael ran his hand over the blaster, feeling secure in holding it.

There was a stir just outside the corridor where he hid. He hugged the wall, but some of the alien people had seen him. They pointed and whispered, fluttering like startled birds. He saw one hopping up and down in queer, excited little jumps. He felt safe. He couldn't believe these soft little people were any real danger to him. They looked too much like frail children. There was a stir at the fringe of the crowd.

Chael tightened his grip on the blaster. He didn't want to use it. He wished belatedly that he'd brought something less lethal. He was sure to kill several if he fired. One of the pastel people pushed through the crowd. He wore a white robe with a wide blue band around the hem. Behind him marched six taller, heavier figures dressed in grey. They were in stark contrast to the fragile onlookers. Chael was sure they were as alien to the cavern as he was himself. Something about their grey uniforms with the ornate badge on the tunic stirred lost memories. They stared for a moment, then the man in the blue-striped robe asked a question in an alien sing-song. The language was meaningless to Chael.

"I don't understand," he said quietly.

The man spoke again, his tone more demanding. Chael shrugged helplessly, but the gesture wasn't understood either. One of the grey figures moved out of position, edging towards Chael's left. The grey ones worried him. They were half a head taller than the pastel people and twice as massive—his own size. They looked tough. The rest of the group moved apart.

Chael watched them warily, his finger on the firing stud. The man in the striped robe moved closer. Chael backed away, but in two steps his back was against the tunnel wall. He wanted to move out into the open. He wasn't about to be trapped into the long chase down the dead end corridor.

One of the grey ones drew a slender silver tube from the pocket of his tunic. It was about the width of Chael's little finger and a hand's length long. He pointed the tube at Chael. Chael aimed the blaster, ready to fire and run, but the alien leader moved first. He took hold of the barrel of Chael's weapon and pulled it towards his chest. Chael tried to shake him off, but the alien was stronger than he looked. Chael stared into his eyes as he tried to free the blaster. He couldn't bring himself to fire. He thought he saw compassion in the thin face. The silver tube buzzed softly, and Chael fell to the floor, unconscious.

2

He awoke lying on a strange bed. It was firm, covered with satin fabric, smooth under his hand. He felt good; warm and relaxed, as if after a vigorous swim.

"Can you understand me now?" the man in the striped robe asked. Chael hadn't noticed him come in.

"Of course," he answered.

"How do you feel?"

"I feel fine," he said. He was having a hard time staying awake.

"Do you have any weapons other than your blaster and knife?"

"Nothing," Chael answered, yawning. He wished the man would let him go back to sleep.

"Rest now," the other said, as if reading his thoughts. "We'll talk again later."

And Chael obeyed.

The next time he woke up, he was alone. Someone had pulled a satin sheet up over him. He still felt good, but the euphoria was gone. He was himself again. He wondered if he'd dreamed he was speaking to the man in the striped robe. But this was the same room. Stretching, he climbed out of bed. He was naked, but he'd worry about finding his clothes and weapons later. He didn't see any door. Three of the walls were of ivory plastic, like the corridor. The fourth was covered with a pale blue rectangle. He examined it but couldn't tell if it was picture, window, or com-screen. The floor was a rubbery, darker blue.

He sat back down on the bed. It was the only piece of furniture in the room. He was beginning to feel hungry and thirsty. Abruptly, a rectangle in the far wall slid aside. Chael rolled across the floor and into attack position before he had time to think. The man in the striped robe blinked at him.

"Good morning," the slender alien said calmly enough. "I'm glad to see that you're awake now."

Somewhat sheepishly, Chael returned to the bed. "I'm fine now," he said, then paused. The man was speaking Chael's own language. "How did you learn . . . ?"

"Your language?" the other interrupted. "Listen more closely. You'll find it's not so."

He was right, Chael realized. The sense was still there, but when he listened closely, he heard the alien syllables.

"That's how the translator works, you see," the other said. "You'll soon get used to it." He sat down on the bed next to Chael. Chael moved back, being so close to someone he didn't know made him uneasy. "My name is Katt," the alien said.

"I'm called Chael, the outlander."

"Then we're friends," Katt said.

Chael raised one dark eyebrow. He didn't quite follow the exchange, but he was willing to go along with Katt's apparent friendliness—until he found out otherwise.

"Who are you?" Chael asked, "and what do you want of me?"

"I am Katt, the Ozine Leader, and I want clarity."

Somehow, Chael wasn't surprised to find himself among the Ozine. Too many details of what he'd seen tallied with the old legends—fragile aliens living within an airless asteroid far from any sun. But for now, he needed to establish his own position.

"Look," he said earnestly, "someone from here was killed last night—burned down. I saw it happen."

"But no one is missing from Ozine Station," Katt protested.

"He used a wand to reach Fenmark," Chael said, "but someone burned him down before he had a chance to get clear. I used the wand to come here." He paused, remembering. There was still no sign of his clothes. "Where are my things? Where's the wand?" he demanded.

"The wand is in a safe place," Katt answered placidly.

"Give it to me," Chael said, suddenly intense. "It's mine."

"You are the finder, not the owner," Katt said. "The wand belongs to the Ozine. But tell me more about this stranger."

"He wasn't Ozine," Chael said flatly. He was out-manuevered for the moment, but he wasn't about to give up. "He wore a grey uniform, like the man who stunned me."

"Like the traders?" Katt said thoughtfully. "The trader Mave and her Household have reported no one missing. In fact, I believe they've just added a new member."

Chael reined in his impatience. If he thought the alien had the wand on him, he would have broken the fragile neck there and then, and run. But Katt had said the wand was in a safe place, wherever that was. He had to find out.

"Who are these traders you're talking about?" Chael asked. He didn't remembering hearing about any people like them, but it had been a long, long time since he'd lived as a Rim Runner. All he had to go on were a child's vague memories.

"Why did they stun me?"

"To keep you from harming us," Katt replied reasonably.

17

So, maybe he'd looked threatening carrying the blaster, they still had no excuse for robbing him. The Ozine were far from being his allies.

". . . . small population," Katt said, apparently reverting to Chael's earlier question, "but highly mobile. Matriarchal . . . . independent Households are intensely competitive but will unite when under attack. We find them useful."

"When can I leave here?" Chael asked impatiently. Already, he felt confined by the windowless room.

"You wish to view Ozine Station?"

"Yes." Anything was better than staying in this cramped cube. He'd get the wand back as soon as he could. In the meantime, maybe he could learn more about how to use it.

"Very well," Katt answered. "Wait here, and I'll arrange for a guide. You'll find food and your clothing in the servo-hatch." He turned and was gone. The door slid shut, solid and impenetrable, behind him.

Chael noticed a small panel had opened in the featureless ivory wall. Inside reposed a tray of steaming food, a pitcher of water, and his uniform. His clothes had been carefully cleaned, then dropped haphazardly, with no attempt to fold them neatly. A quick search through them revealed his father's navigator's medallion, still intact. Thankfully, he put it on. He dressed rapidly. The uniform fit closely enough to keep him from looking too rumpled. His knife and blaster were gone, along with the wand.

The food was good, he decided after he tasted it, some kind of salty-sweet bread and a slightly sour fruit. The pitcher contained pure water, so far as he could tell. He drank most of it. Katt returned shortly after Chael finished eating. He had another of the pastel people with him.

"I am Sinshee," the newcomer said. She had tightly curled black hair and golden eyes. She waited expectantly.

He remembered Katt's earlier greeting. "My name is Chael," he replied, wondering just what he was committing himself to. Sinshee smiled, and Katt looked relieved. He'd passed the first test. Although how they could expect him to know their ways . . . .

"I will be your friend and your guide," Sinshee said, taking his right hand. Her fingers were small and brittle.

Over the next few days, she was with him constantly, showing him all the marvels of Ozine Station.

"These are the stim vats," Sinshee said as they entered yet another cavernous room. Chael saw row after row of shining tanks. The ceiling was webbed with tubing and catwalks, and a dozen Ozine tended the vats. A sharp, spicy odor filled the air. It was odd but not unpleasant.

"Stim?" asked Chael. "What's that?"

"Stim. Itself," Sinshee snapped. "We make it." They stared at one another, the thin thread of communication once more broken despite the efforts of the translator. Perhaps if he knew more about the mechanics of the thing, he'd be able to use it better. It was worth a try.

"How does the translator work?" he asked.

"It translates," Sinshee said unhelpfully. "How else should it work?" She was clearly giving the best answer she could.

Something was wrong here, Chael thought. A people who gave non-answers to even the simplest technical questions couldn't have built this complex—or the wand. He had to find someone who knew more.

19

"Let's talk about the traders," he said, watching the attendants thread their way through the catwalks above the vats.

"I've exchanged names with the chief trader's brother, Jody," Sinshee said, as if that were all there was to say.

"But where are they? I haven't seen a sign of the traders during this whole tour" Chael persisted. Getting information from one of the Ozine required all the patience he possessed.

"They're in their own section," Sinshee said. "You asked to see the Ozine."

"Well, now I'd like to see the traders," Chael said, keeping his voice soft and slow.

Sinshee shrugged and led him on another long walk until they came to a wide corridor that looked just like many others they'd passed.

"Here we are," Sinshee said.

Looking more closely, Chael saw a red band painted around the circumference. It was the only thing that seemed to demark the traders' quarters.

"No one around," he said. "Do they always hide?"

"The Dann must be back," Sishee answered. "The traders go to the control room then." She took Chael's hand in her own and tugged him along with surprising strength. "Come on."

They crossed the red line, and Sinshee led him down a wide main corridor. The walls were painted in brightly colored geometric designs, and bas-relief cornices overhung the doorways. Chael would have liked time to study them more closely, but Sinsheee urged him on, claiming the traders' art made her head ache. At length, they reached the control room. It was a large, open space, some twenty meters across; ample, but not so vast as some of Ozine Station's echoing caverns. Chael recognized almost familiar computer equipment. The majority seemed to be weapons systems. There were about a dozen people in the room. Most wore the grey uniforms he'd seen before. But when he glanced to the far end of the room, his eyes were drawn to a tall, striking woman dressed in pale blue. She issued a stream of orders that were quickly obeyed. Chael sensed tension in the room. Who or what were the Dann? he wondered. Sinshee seemed oblivious to the atmosphere. Blandly, she brought him over to the chief trader.

"Here is a stranger who desires your friendship," she began formally.

Mave noticed them for the first time. "What!"

"Here is a stranger," Sinshee began again.

"Blast you!" Mave swore. "You Ozine have no sense at all. Can't you see we're under attack?" She turned to the nearest grey-uniformed trader. "Have someone get them out of here." Her attention snapped back to the tank in front of her, her knuckles white as her hands gripped the edge. Chael saw sparks of red and gold in the dark blue battle tank. As he watched, three of the red ships converged on a single gold defender. It flared briefly and disappeared.

"Andin!" Mave exclaimed. But she forced herself under rigid control, pushing away her grief and seeming to grow icily cold. Chael nodded approvingly. No one could command a battle without having self-command first. But the engagement did not go well. If the battle tank followed the standard pattern, then the red sparks of the attackers outnumbered the traders' ships by three to one. Mave looked up suddenly.

"Are you here still? I ordered these Ozine removed."

"I'm not Ozine," Chael insisted. All his training urged him to join in the defense. He wasn't used to watching passively while someone else did his fighting for him, but his protest did him no good.

"You're not trader either," Mave said, "and that makes you of no use to me. Jody!"

A young man appeared. He was no more than twenty, Chael guessed, and he had Mave's red hair and green eyes.

"Come with me, please," he said. "This is no time for strangers to visit the control room."

But the floor trembled as the Dann laser cannon scored a hit on Ozine Station. The lights faltered, then flickered back on. Gravel and fist-sized chunks of rock rained from the ceiling to clatter on instrument pannels. Jody fell to his knees, his hands to his head. Chael dragged the boy's arm across his shoulders and pulled him up. The young trader seemed dazed, and blood trickled from a cut on his forehead. He leaned heavily on Chael.

"The shields are going," Jody gasped. The room vibrated under another blast, and more rock fell. A long crack split the wall near them.

"Come on," Chael said. He pulled the boy towards a more stable corner. Sinshee trailed behind, protesting at the noise.

"They've been harassing us for months," Jody said as Chael helped him to rest against an undamaged section of wall. "But Sullat has united all the Dann, and she's sent a full squadron against us this time."

The room rocked again, and Chael heard distant booming. More rock fell from the ceiling, in great chunks this time. A boulder brushed by his head, and he was half buried in a shower of gravel. He struggled to free himself, sliding on the loose stones. Jody and Sinshee were lost in the clouds of dust. Choking, he wiped at his tearing eyes.

"Get me another gunner!" he heard Mave order.

"There's no one left," another voice answered hoarsely.

Chael tripped and stumbled into an unseen figure. Strong hands grabbed him. He looked up at Mave.

"You again!" she exclaimed. "Well, not-Ozine, can you handle a laser cannon?"

"I'm a soldier of the Fenmark," Chael answered. "Your weapons are close enough to standard."

"They're Ozine-made," she said. "Any child can operate one. Just make sure you can fire when you have the Dann in your sights."

Chael nodded. He wouldn't freeze like some un-blooded novice. The console Mave assigned him was simple, as she'd said. It had a smaller version of the battle tank mounted above the controls. Chael saw red fireflys swarming over gold. All he had to do was line up the cross-hairs on the scope and pull the trigger, but the red fireflys danced alarmingly, and the gold ships moved recklessly under the cross-hairs. It took a few tries, but he soon got the hang of it. He out-guessed the erratic red pinpoints and caused half-a-dozen to wink out on his scope.

The dust in the control room thickened. Chael coughed and wiped off his screen with his right hand. Sweat trickled down his neck and into his eyes. The red lights were disappearing, moving off the edge of his scope. He sat tensed, waiting for them to reappear.

"The battle is over. The Dann have retreated," Mave said. She stood just behind him, sounding ex-hausted. She was covered with dust, and her uniform stuck to her in damp patches. Chael smelled the sweat and some lingering perfume. It suddenly made her a real person for him, not just another commanding of-ficer. On the screen, eight gold lights moved together. There'd been more than a dozen when he started.

"Your losses are heavy," he said.

"Six of my Household," she agreed. "I will grieve for them."

"I'm sorry."

"You've done well, not-Ozine. Without your help, there would be even more dead."

Chael was silent. He felt weak and lightheaded. Jody appeared next to Mave. The trader youth looked at him with concern. Chael glanced down and noticed the blood running from his leg. He felt nothing. Mave looked at his leg, then into his eyes.

"My name is Chael," he said, suddenly desperate that someone should care whether he lived or died.

"t'Verra Mave, chief . . . ." But the rest was lost. The floor was soft as he fell against it.

3

Chael awoke slowly, wondering why the ceiling of his barracks room was painted with red and blue stripes. Then he remembered: Ozine Station and the traders' sector.

"He's awake now," he heard a woman say. Startling blue eyes that matched his own bent near him. With a shock, Chael saw that even the dark ring around the iris was the same. It had been years since he'd seen eyes like that outside of a mirror. Their owner smiled at him, and he noticed that she had creamy skin and blonde braids pinned high on her head. Then Jody appeared in his line of vision.

"Just relax," the boy said. "You're still in trader quarters."

Chael ignored the advice and tried to sit up. He

made it half way, but his skin prickled, and the edges of his vision went grey. The woman caught him as he fell.

"Take it easy!" she said. "You've lost a lot of blood." Gently, she lowered him back onto the pillows. Chael's leg began throbbing, and memory came back.

"The battle? We won?"

"Yes," Jody told him. "It cost us, but we won. You caught a chunk of metal in your leg. We used a healing ray, and it's nearly all right, but we couldn't do much about the shock."

"I've been hurt worse," Chael said gruffly, wiggling his leg to see if all the tendons were intact. Everything seemed all right.

"We're grateful for your help," the woman said, smoothing the blanket as if he were a child. But somehow, Chael couldn't find the words to protest the unsoldierly attentions. "Without you, many more of the Household would have died."

Chael felt acutely uncomfortable. The women he'd known on Fenmark were either officers' wives who seldom spoke to an outlander soldier, or else they were camp followers, far more interested in the credits in his pockets than in Chael the man. This woman with the ice-blue eyes was outside his experience.

She smiled again, showing white, even teeth. "But we haven't exchanged names. That Ozine custom is the only thing I like about this Station. I'm t'Verra Lissa." She bowed with an air of teasing mockery.

"Behave yourself, Lissa," Jody said. "The man will think you're serious." He bowed in turn. "My name is t'Verra Jody."

"I'm called Chael of the Fenmark," he said, forgetting for a moment that he was a man with no allegiance.

"Could you use some food, Chael?" Jody asked.

Chael nodded, feeling suddenly ravenous.

"Just so you take it slow and easy," Lissa warned. "It's been a couple of days since you've had anything solid."

Jody left, and Chael took the opportunity to look at the room more closely. He would rather have looked at Lissa, but he didn't want to make a fool of himself by staring at her so, instead, he examined the painted walls and a carved animal in dark wood. The silence was growing uncomfortable when the chief trader herself carried in his tray.

"Jody tells me you're awake and hungry," she said as she sat beside his bed. She put the tray down on a small table nearby. "I take that as a good sign."

"Thanks," Chael said. "I'll live." He felt embarrassed by all the attention.

Mave smiled. "We had our doubts." She wore a clean blue jumpsuit, and her tunic had the badge of her Household embroidered in gold just above her left breast. The light blue color set off her red hair.

"I'll leave him in your hands," Lissa said. "I have some other work to catch up on." She left quickly, and Chael was sorry to see her go.

"Don't look so glum," Mave said. "She'll be back."

He looked dismayed. "Am I that obvious?"

"Eat your lunch and don't worry about it," she advised. "Lissa hasn't been with us long, but I can see she's taken with you."

Chael dropped the subject and went to work on the food. Still, he wasn't displeased.

"Your friend Sinshee has gone back to the Ozine sector," Mave said a little later.

"Look, I'm sorry about the way Sinshee barged in on you in the middle of an attack."

26

"Well," she said shrugging, "the Ozine are like that. In their own way, they're even more alien than the Dann."

Chael finished the last bite of food. He felt much stronger, and his curiosity was aroused. "Who and what are the Dann?" he asked, settling back among the pillows again. During the battle he'd fought automatically, because he was under attack, but now he needed to know more.

"Who are the Dann? Chael, you must be a stranger indeed," the chief trader exclaimed, her elegant russet eyebrows raised in surprise.

"Mave," he said, using her name for the first time, "I'm so far from home that I don't even know what quadrant I'm in."

"How is this?"

So he explained to her about the stranger and the wand, but he left out most of his life on Fenmark and the story of his Rim Runner parents. Some things were private.

"So the stranger used a wand," she said thoughtfully when he'd finished. "And then you used it."

"I had to," he said simply.

"Chael, you're follhardy. For all you knew, you were throwing yourself into an armed camp."

"Even that would be better than rotting in the governor's palace. That's no life, with every day exactly like the one before it," he said bitterly.

"How strange you are. All life repeats itself, but you want to be the one man who lives to a random pattern," Mave said studying him thoughtfully, as if he were indeed some alien species.

"You haven't told me about the Dann," he said, tired of trying to explain himself.

"It's a short story," she replied, leaning forward so that the light glinted copper in her hair. "During

27

the Hassad wars, a hospital ship crashed on Iradii IV. The ship carried wounded and dying troops, exhausted medics, and a minimum of supplies. Iradii IV was hostile, with an atmosphere full of deadly radiation.''

She shrugged eloquently. ''Many of them died during the first few days. The ones who survived lived by old laws. Iradii was a jungle world, and the Dann became jungle animals. That was nearly 2000 years ago. Now, they have a more stable society, a more advanced technology, and unfortunately for the rest of us, an expanding population. They need land. The League has it, and the Dann mean to take it for themselves. They still live by jungle laws, for all their veneer of civilization.''

They were interrupted by a rapid pad of soft-soled boots in the corridor. Jody burst in.

''Mave,'' he said breathlessly, ''the Dann want to parley.''

''To Parley?''

''They want to land a freighter on Ozine Station. The fight damaged their mother ship, and they say they want to be allowed to buy supplies from the Ozine in return for a promise to leave the Station in peace.''

''Meaning until they can regroup,'' Mave said. ''However, we could use some time to recover ourselves. The control room is a shambles. It would also give us an opportunity to study the Dann at first hand.'' She paused thoughtfully. ''Well, we can talk anyway. The rest I'll have to consider very carefully.''

Jody left to convey her message.

''Can the Ozine provide food for the Dann?'' Chael asked.

''The Ozine can make anything,'' Mave assured him, ''but they charge dearly for it. Why do you think we're doing business in hyperdrive ships, instead of using the wands? A key to the silver door would cost the income of a dozen worlds. In any case, there were only three made. One belongs to the Regency of Rall, one is in the grave of the divine philosopher Duvall, and the third was lost during the rebellion of the Xichi, or so it was thought.''

Chael was silent. A dozen worlds . . . and Mave wasn't the sort to exaggerate. He had to get that wand back from Katt. For him, it meant freedom.

''But I have work to do,'' Mave said, rising. ''Jody will need help.''

''What about the Ozine?'' Chael asked. ''Aren't you going to notify them?''

''The Ozine will not be interested,'' Mave replied as she left. Remembering Sinshee's behavior during the attack, Chael was forced to agree with her.

The reception committee was small: Mave, Jody, and somehow, Chael, too. The rest of the Household waited in the control room. The welcoming committee donned space suits for their expedition to Ozine Station's airless exterior, but they were unlike any suits Chael had ever seen. Consisting of a belt with a simple catch, when the catch was fastened, the wearer was enveloped in a pale mist, like frost. Chael's companions looked ghostly, as did what he could see of himself, but they apparently were used to the frost-effect and ignored it.

''Here she comes,'' Jody said. A white streak flashed half across the sky, then stopped. It became a circle of light that grew as it descended. Chael felt a stir of the same excitement that always gripped him at the sight of a starship. Red and blue lights blinked rapidly along its sides. One by one, they shut off. The hatch opened in the underbelly, and Chael had his first glimpse of the Dann. They tumbled out, a grotesque mixture that his eyes at first refused to make sense of.

Those mutations had to be due to more than radiation. Some of the changes were deliberate.

Mave stepped forward. "Welcome," she said, and the formal greetings to an enemy at truce began. Chael felt uneasy having the Dann so close when they'd so recently been trying to kill him. This wasn't the way war was fought on Fenmark. He watched the visitors as carefully as if they were Coss raiders.

Tall and short, two-armed, four-armed, grotesque, beautiful, bloated with organs whose function he didn't understand, the Dann were unlike anything he'd ever seen. Chael stared, fascinated by their variety. It was as if each Dann were determined to be as unlike any other as possible. A bloated, furry being rolled by him, followed by a brisk stick-man. Chael hurriedly looked back to the Dann captain. He at least seemed almost normal, although he sported a second set of arms and an oddly lengthened skull. The Dann captain took off his jeweled collar and placed it around Mave's neck. It seemed to mark the end of the ceremony.

So they were all friends now, Chael thought skeptically. Still, he for one would watch his back. At last, the procession moved again. Chael and Jody fell in behind Mave as she led the small party of Dann into the trader sector.

". . . lost 60% of our stores," the Dann captain was saying as Chael took off his belt. "We can't make it back to Iradii without restocking."

"You've already killed six of my Household," Mave said coldly. "I won't help you murder the rest, Captain Henyab."

"Consider the consequences if we can't leave," Henyab said. His voice held its own flat menace.

Yes, Chael thought, consider the consequences. One more battle like the last and there wouldn't be any traders to worry about. He was disgusted with all this pussyfooting diplomacy. Didn't Mave realize what she was letting them in for?

"Why not let them starve?" he asked Jody. "They'll be back at our throats in no time."

"This one squadron is nothing to Sullatt," Jody answered. "It's a test of strength. The real battle comes when the League sends its protest."

"But don't you care? Your people died in that 'test.'"

Jody turned a suddenly fierce face towards him. "Of course I care," he said hotly. "But there's nothing we can do. The traders play this whole game on bluff. We don't have any squadrons in reserve." He turned away abruptly, knowing he'd said too much.

Chael regarded his retreating back thoughtfully. Just how weak were the traders? he wondered. Backed by the League, they should be able to handle anything the Dann could come up with. The League—the League of Human Worlds—to give it its full title, was rich enough, powerful enough to crush any opposition. Or so he'd been taught in the academy on Fenmark. The semi-barbaric Dann should be no match for them—unless the League had its own reasons for being slack in its support of the traders. Chael felt that he was getting into a political struggle that was out of his depth, but like Jody, there was nothing he could do.

Mave and the Dann captain had settled down to the serious business of negotiating. Chael felt restless. Thinking of the Ozine made him think of Katt and Sinshee. Had Katt found out anything new? Had Sinshee missed him? he wondered. He decided now was a good time to find out. The conference looked like dragging on for hours. He moved up next to Jody.

"I'm going back to Ozine territory," he said quietly. Jody nodded, and Chael left. The corridors were all but deserted as he made his way out of the trader sector. Everyone was with the Dann. Almost everyone, he amended as he passed Lissa on guard duty at the entrance. She smiled warmly at him as he left. He smiled back but was too absorbed in his own problems to talk.

"But what can I do?" Chael asked, exasperated. Katt had gotten no further with his investigation. He still insisted that no one was missing, and now he'd brought up the vexing topic of how Chael was to pay for his keep. The Ozine economy was small and closed, he said. They couldn't afford a permanent guest, and they couldn't afford to send him away either. Chael didn't understand the economics, but he did know that the Ozine had no use for a soldier—or so they claimed.

"The vats are the only thing you're qualified to work on," Katt said reasonably. "You don't have the training for any more skilled work."

Angrily, Chael ran his hands through his dark hair. There was no place for him anywhere. If he could, he'd have shaken the wand out of the alien's possession, but the Ozine Leader doubtless had it well hidden. Abruptly, he left Katt and wandered restlessly through the Station. He couldn't face the blank, ivory cell that was his room, but he didn't want to talk to the Ozine either.

Even if he worked at the vats, he thought, it would barely pay for his keep. From what Katt said, he'd never earn enough to get off Ozine Station. He felt hopeless, trapped. He passed by twittering groups of Ozine, by Ozine workers tending the stim vats, by a solitary Ozine staring vacantly as the stim pushed his brain into high gear. Chael found it hard to believe that lofty thoughts were going on behind that idiot mask, but Katt insisted it was so. The stim acted directly on the Ozine neural centers, increasing their intelligence geometrically. At length, Chael noticed he was near Sinshee's quarters. He'd never been inside before, but she'd pointed them out to him. On impulse, he decided to see her. She was the closest thing to a friend he had. He stood in front of her door and called her name. He called twice before she answered.

"Chael, you're back!" She opened the door for him at once. "Come in. Are you well now?" She seemed to regard the Dann attack and his injury as a minor inconvenience.

"Well enough," Chael answered, although he wasn't so sure at the moment. He wondered if he'd ever get used to the Ozine way of looking at things.

"Sit here," Sinshee said, patting a large yellow cushion. She dropped down on the half opposite him.

"Would you like something to eat or drink?"

"Nothing," Chael said. Now that he was inside, he felt it had been a mistake to come here. He was drawn very taut. Sinshee wore a yellow robe that matched the cushion and set off her golden Ozine eyes. Her hair was arranged in a complicated pattern of braids and knots. She looked more than ever alien, yet disturbingly desirable.

"Have I offended you?" she asked. "You look at me strangely."

"No, not you. I've just had some bad news, and I don't know what to do about it," Chael admitted.

"What's so bad?" Sinshee asked sympathetically.

Her sympathy was like a goad to Chael's furious frustration. "I can't stay here, and I can't leave, but I'm not going to be chained to some mindless routine," he burst out. "I want my freedom!"

"Of course you'll be free," Sinshee said, putting her delicate hand on his shoulder. His anger seemed to have no effect on her. He looked at her helplessly.

33

He'd never make her understand. Abruptly, she kissed him, and he kissed her back, absently at first, then with more passion. He was very lonely. Suddenly, he started and withdrew his hand.

"Chael, what's wrong?" Sinshee asked anxiously.

"You!" Chael exclaimed. "You're male!"

Sinshee looked confused. "But all Ozine are male. There hasn't been a female born to our people in four generations. All our race must breed in the tanks until the Regenetrix comes."

"I didn't know," Chael said, confused in turn. He stood up slowly. He was overcome with a longing to be back in his barracks on Fenmark.

"Where are you going?"

"I don't know," he said. He looked down on Sinshee. "I'll explain some other time." He was gone before the Ozine could protest.

He prowled restlessly through Ozine Station, not caring where he went. Most of the ivory corridors were deserted. There were never many Ozine about. Maybe there weren't many Ozine at all, Chael thought. Perhaps that was why Katt was so sure of his census and why he was so insistent that Chael earn his keep. It made no difference. There was no way off Ozine Station. He was trapped. And Ozine Station was dead, an airless asteroid riddled with tunnels.

The way before him opened out into another of the caverns the Station's builders seemed to favor. It was filled with silence, the echo of times long gone. The far end of the cavern was unfinished. Rough grey rock rose like stair-steps to the crystal dome above. He climbed. The coarse grey rock rubbed his hand raw, but he ignored the pain. He ignored everything but his need to climb, to get away from this alien world that had suddenly become his prison.

Parsecs away, on a planet in the grip of ice and

barbarism, the Wolf-witch rose from her fire. Her vision was true. The War Leader drew nearer. Chanting, she made magic to bring him to her people. The flames crackled in reply, throwing golden reflections off her naked body.

4

Chael didn't know how long he perched at the base of the dome, but it seemed that hours had passed when he heard the scrape of boots on the rocks below him and the harsh, steady breathing of someone else making the climb. He sat quietly, half hoping the climber would fail to see him wedged into a niche among the rocks. He stared out across the cavern, his mind a jumble of formless thoughts. The climber drew up onto the ledge beside him. He turned coldly and was relieved to see that it wasn't one of the Ozine. Mave sat next to him, panting a little as she caught her breath.

"Why have you come?" he asked.

"Katt said you should be ready to come down about now," she answered. "And he said you probably wouldn't want to see any of his people for a while."

"Katt said . . . ? And how does he know all this?" Chael asked belligerently.

"The Ozine know most things," Mave replied: "At least when they're high on stim, and Katt is about to go full phase."

There was another long silence, but it was a companionable pause. Chael began to feel more hopeful.

"If you're tired of the Ozine, you're welcome in the trader sector," Mave said. "My Household is low. With six dead in the attack, we need new people."

"In your Household?"

"You'd have to swear an oath of fealty to me, and I'd be responsible for your well-being." She waited expectantly.

"I don't know," Chael said. Binding himself to the traders seemed just as much a dead end as working for the Ozine. If the opportunity came to leave Ozine Station, he wanted to be free to go.

"Think on it," Mave said. She stood up. "In the meantime, there's food and wine waiting in the traders' sector. Will you come there with me?"

Chael realized that he was hungry and thirsty and had had enough of being alone. "Why not?"

The climb down was difficult, and the stones lacerated his already tender hand.

"I should have brought gloves for you," Mave said. She wore blue gloves herself, but they were obviously much too small for him. She had her second wind now and was breathing easily.

"No matter," Chael said. But the mention of gloves caused him to remember the single dark grey glove he'd found in the tunnel—a glove such as one of Mave's Household might wear. Mave had shown him a great deal of kindness, but he was a loner by nature. He resolved to do some investigating himself, beginning among the Household. He could ask all the questions he wanted under the pretext of thinking of joining.

"Hold!" Mave cried as he missed his footing and started to slide. Her strong grip arrested his fall. He grasped the rock with his metal hand and noticed the play of silver cables for the first time in days. He knew Mave must have seen it, but she showed no reaction.

"We're almost to the bottom," she said encouragingly.

"Good." He ignored the cramps in his legs. Mave talked as they descended, as much to keep her mind off how high up they were, he suspected, as to cheer him up. Well, he was grateful for her efforts. The climb ended finally, and Mave stopped to apply some soothing ointment from a tiny med-kit in her belt.

"Do you ever talk about what happened to your other hand?" she asked.

Chael stiffened and withdrew his good right hand from her grasp.

"Never," he said.

She nodded, as if she understood, and Chael regretted his abruptness. He held out his right hand again for her to finish smoothing on the ointment.

"I'm sorry," he said. "Maybe some time, but not now."

"All right," she agreed. On the way back to the traders' sector, she brought up a new topic.

"Katt agreed to fulfill the terms of the settlement before he went into full phase," she said soberly. "The supplies will be ready for the Dann within two cycles."

"But why give them anything?" Chael asked again. "You could wipe out this squadron, if you attacked now."

"Chael, I see that you come from a pragmatic people." She sighed. "We could do it, perhaps, but the gain would be only temporary and the loss far-reaching." They were in the traders' sector now, and she turned down a corridor Chael hadn't been in before. She opened the door.

"My quarters," she said, gesturing towards a chair.

The shape was odd, but it looked comfortable. "Will you have some wine?" She stood before a heavily carved cabinet. Chael nodded, and she poured two glasses of dark red wine. They sipped without a toast. She sat on the sofa opposite him.

"So," she continued, "your very practical suggestion won't work for one reason."

"Being?" The wine had a spicy, cider-like taste. Chael decided he liked it.

"We're weak, Chael." She waved aside his protest. "Oh, I know that it doesn't look that way from here, but I assure you, it's true. We're a small, scattered people. There aren't more than a few thousand Households, and they're spread across all the known worlds. We have only one city."

"We're far richer than we allow most people to know, but we are weak. We have no armies, no land, no industry, and few people. We survive only because we are necessary." She paused to take another drink from her glass. "We are the only ones the members of the League can trust." She smiled ironically. "We convey diplomatic messages, arbitrate disputes, and trade in lightweight, high-value merchandise—all without let or hindrance, on any world in the League. We watch Ozine Station because no one else can be trusted to do so." She looked at him earnestly from over the top of her glass. Her eyes were like emeralds.

"The Ozine are dying, a remnant of what they once were—long before humanity ever entered space—but they still know enough secrets to make them dangerous. Not because they'd use them against us, but because they have no interest in what's done with their toys once they've sold them."

"But the Dann attacked you," Chael said. "What about them?"

Mave frowned. "The Dann are barbarians, and a

law unto themselves. They hope to take over this Station, and so control the Ozine—and their secrets. With the aid of Ozine technology, they could take over the entire League. But the Ozine themselves refuse to have more than my Household to guard them. They say,'' she looked at him as if challenging him to disbelieve her, ''they say that it would prevent the return of the Regenetrix. They claim they've learned this through the stim.''

''What do they mean, 'Regenetrix?' '' Chael demanded. ''Sinshee mentioned it too, and she—he claimed that all Ozine are male, that they breed artificially.''

Mave nodded. ''That's true, in so far as it goes. The Ozine have no females. They reproduce by stimulating growth in male sperm cells, but the process is degenerative. There are fewer and fewer Ozine born each cycle, and they are always male. They're a dying race, Chael, but they have a myth, a prophesy, if you will. Before the end overtakes them, the Regenetrix will appear, a female Ozine who will rule this Station and renew the race.''

''But if they can't breed females, where will she come from?''

Mave shrugged. ''They don't know, or won't say. It's all part of something they've learned while using stim.''

''The Ozine claim a lot of great thoughts when they're under the influence of stim,'' Chael said.

''Indeed, they do,'' Mave agreed. ''Stim has been tested on human volunteers—although the Ozine warned us not to try it.''

''Warned you not to?''

''The Ozine are alien, both mentally and physically—far more so than they appear to be,'' she said. ''For them, the stim provides a marvelous period of

39

heightened mental powers with no unpleasant after-effects. But it's different for us. The human volunteers also reported a wonderful expansion of their mental powers—if they lived through the withdrawal—but they could never remember exactly what any of these marvelous ideas were afterward. The withdrawal seemed to wipe out all earlier memories, up to the point of taking the stim. So, we had what appeared to be a useless and dangerous drug for human beings.'' She stopped to refill both their glasses. ''At first, we didn't realize just how dangerous.''

''What happened?'' Chael asked. He sensed carefully controlled bitterness in Mave's tone.

''There were three volunteers in the original experiment, all first class students. One died during withdrawal. The other two seemed normal enough, but remained at the testing center for observation. Ten days after the experiment, the testing center lab was broken into. Nothing was taken but the rest of the stim. They found Vickor dead in the fields behind the center. He'd died within a few minutes of taking the second dose.''

''What about the third volunteer?''

She smiled ironically. ''I was more fortunate. I lived, and I developed no addiction. The trader genetic pattern has drifted away from the League norm—that may have been what saved me. It was shortly after the experiment that the Ozine contacted the testing center. They insisted that I, and I alone, guard Ozine Station.''

She fell silent. Chael was sure that this was something she'd been brooding on for a long time. In her own way, Mave was as much caught in the trap of Ozine Station as he was.

''So we're at a standstill,'' he said finally. ''We can't act against the Dann, and we can't give up Ozine Station.''

"Precisely."

Chael stifled a yawn. The wine and fatigue were catching up with him. Mave noticed at once.

"Come," she said rising gracefully. "I'll show you to your quarters." She led him to yet another ivory cubicle.

"Don't the Ozine ever change?" Chael asked, looking around.

"Not if they can help it," she replied as she left him. The chief trader was going to be here a long, long time, he reflected as he undressed. She knew it, and he didn't think she liked it.

Three days later, they loaded the last of the supplies onto the Dann transport. Chael felt dissatisfied. He hadn't found out anything new about the mysterious stranger who'd died before his eyes. He'd even gone back to the tunnel to examine it again, but nothing distinguished it from the hundreds of other half-finished, abandoned corridors in Ozine Station. It was as if the workers had simply walked off the job and never come back, leaving the machinery to gather dust where it sat. Which, he thought as he wrestled with a particularly awkward crate, led to another odd fact. The Ozine had no machines. Not in use. Not what he'd call machines. The excavators were long abandoned. There was no mechanical transportation. One walked in Ozine Station. There was nothing to ride, and there was no way, save muscle power, of loading these bulky crates of supplies. The Ozine, it seemed, had either "magic" or nothing.

His footsteps rang loudly in the hollow interior of the Dann transport. He still distrusted the Dann and thought supplying them was a mistake. He had the same feeling of impending danger that had saved him before on the borders of Fenmark. Trouble was coming: he didn't know how or from where, but he wished he had his blaster. He couldn't think of a way to end the stalemate, not within the parameters of the traders' politics. Mave moved skillfully, but the enemy was too powerful. Chael admired the chief trader, but he prefered a woman who was more yielding. Like Lissa, he thought, watching her direct the loading. She smiled at him, and he felt warmed.

"Save your tricks for someone else, sister. I'm not impressed." Kemmet stepped disdainfully past the smokey fire where the stim leaves burned. Her white dress and copper ornaments were in marked contrast to her sister's wiry, naked body.

"I don't deal in tricks," Ona replied, "and whether you believe in the power of the wolf or not makes no difference. The power is real, and I control it." She rose with dignity and drew her wolfskin cape around her. Kemmet might be the chief's wife, but she was still ignorant of the true source of power.

"The War Leader is coming," Ona announced. "The net is cast. It remains only to draw him in. Already, the events that will carry him here begin."

Chael followed Jody back to the traders' common room. He still felt a nagging worry, but there was nothing he could act on. He rubbed his neck, trying to ease the tense muscles there. They entered the common room together, and Chael was surprised to see it filled with Dann. Somehow, he'd expected them to be back aboard their ship by now. He saw Mave and Lissa in the center of a group of Dann, engaged in some sort of farewell ceremony.

Jody joined them, but Chael hung back. The traders were soon surrounded. Chael's impulse was to stay out of range. His sense of impending danger was

stronger than ever. The Dann pressed closer. Chael
didn't like it. Warily, he circled the room, moving
towards a big, square couch. The couch was mounted
on glides, so it could be moved out of the way for
games. The Dann captain reached to clasp Mave's
hand in a gesture of good will. His other hand flashed
up with a knife.

Mave jerked back, but Chael saw blood on her face.
Jody grabbed her as she fell. Chael, in a cold rage,
sent the massive couch crashing into the Dann. He
saw Lissa fall, but he had no chance to help her. The
low rumble of Dann voices filled the room like thunder. In the distance, he heard the yells of the traders
as they fought,

''Damn politics!'' He swore as he searched frantically for Mave. He saw nothing but the tangle of Dann
and trader combatants as the melee grew in front of
him. He leapt on a table to avoid a Dann knife. He
kicked out and grabbed the knife as it fell. From the
table, he saw Jody pulling Mave out the doorway on
the far side of the room. They were both spattered
with blood. He had time to note that Mave had a Dann
knife and Jody a broken chair leg for a club. Then a
long-limbed, double-jointed Dann cut at his legs, and
Chael was too busy defending his life to watch them
any more.

He slashed back at the Dann with his captured knife.
They fell back before him, but he was tiring rapidly.
He saw a corridor nearby and plunged into it. The way
in front was clear, but the Dann were close behind.
There was a sudden flash and sizzle, and the wall at
his side was marred by a long, black streak. Someone
had a blaster, Chael realized, wishing futilely for his
own. He was panting; he couldn't get enough air. His
legs were leaden. He'd already tired himself hauling
heavy crates.

There was another, closer blast. Then the adrenalin rush hit him, and he took off at double speed. He made for the stim vats. They offered the only cover in Ozine Station. He cursed the Ozine penchant for spartan simplicity. There just weren't enough places to hide.

There was the stim room, straight ahead. Half-a-dozen Ozine in full phase sat or lay about the room. A blaster bolt burned within a finger's width of one of them, but he didn't even flinch. Probably calculated it would miss, Chael thought, as he climbed the nearest inspection ladder. If he could just make it into the maze of pipes and wiring above the vats . . . . Briefly, he wished the Ozine were good for something besides thought. He could use a few allies about now. Once on the catwalk, he hugged the shadows. The Dann were just entering. They looked small and innocent below him, except for Henyab who carried a deadly-looking blaster.

"Spread out and search the place," Henyab ordered. "He can't have gone far." The others hurried to obey. What would they do without their leader? Chael wondered. The captain moved into position just beneath him, and Chael fell prey to temptation. He knew he couldn't excape. The most he could hope for was to make his capture a costly undertaking. The traders had been taken by surprise and put up no effective resistance. They were unarmed and had no proper training in hand-to-hand combat; a straight forward punch on the jaw was more their style. It wasn't much use against knives and blasters. But if he could take the Dann captain out, leave the Dann leaderless, then maybe the traders would have a chance. It wouldn't do to be too hasty. The Dann weren't fools.

The Dann captain moved constantly, searching the shadows. Chael had to get Henyab in the right spot, then distract his attention for a few crucial seconds in order for his desperate plan to work. Getting crisped to ash in mid-fall wouldn't help anyone. Time was running short. A green-skinned, many-eyed Dann was already climbing the access ladder opposite where Chael hid. He would be spotted any moment.

Tensely, Chael crouched. His hand bumped against a long cable of plastic tubing. It jiggled violently, startling him. The Dann on the other side of the room turned suspiciously at the motion, but failed to see Chael. Then Henyab moved into the perfect position, and stood still, staring at the other Dann. Chael was sure he'd never get a better chance. The Dann across the room carried a blaster, but Chael hoped he'd hold his fire for fear of hitting his captain.

Deliberately this time, Chael jerked the tube. It danced wildly, and the Dann's startled exclamation drew the captain's attention. Silently, Chael gathered himself and leapt. But the Dann on the far side saw him and shouted a warning. The Captain whirled, and Chael had just time to see the expression of surprise on his face. Blaster bolts crackled nearby, but none hit them. Chael landed awkwardly. The captain was far stronger than Chael imagined, and the extra pair of arms gave him a decided advantage. They rolled together on the ground, growling like animals. There was another crack of blaster fire above then, and a hot, heavy rain of stim gushed from the ruptured tank. Chael was drenched in it. It poured out faster and faster as the rupture widened from internal pressure.

The Dann seemed to be moving more and more slowly. His actions were childishly obvious. Minutes seemed to drag by between blows. Chael grew bored. His attention was caught by the shiny, reflective surface of one of the big stim vats. Now there was an interesting problem, he thought. Which was real? The reflection or the thing reflected? His thoughts spun off

45

into contemplation of the multitude of dimensions. The matrix of space-time reality spread out before him, and he gazed in awe at the beautiful, perfect complexity of it.

The Dann captain dragged himself up to stare at the silent, slack-jawed face. The stim had no effect on his mutated metabolism.

"You want him killed, captain?"

Henyab considered. "No," he said finally. "He's gone into full phase. If he lives, he may have something useful to tell us. Put him with the others."

5

"Chael, wake up!" Jody urged, shaking the outlander until the other's head rattled lose on his neck. It was no use. The tan, fine-boned face remained slack. Chael was too full of stim to even know where he was, let alone help them.

"It's no good," he said, releasing the one-armed soldier. He looked at Mave, and his heart tore within him. Fair at best, the face she turned to him now was deathly white. A swollen red bruise covered one temple, and there were brownish streaks of dried blood on her cheek.

She opened her eyes, green as his own. "Give him time," she said, her voice a whisper. "He may yet come back to us."

"We haven't got time," Jody said in exasperation.

"The Dann will . . . ." His voice trailed off, and he turned away, angry with himself for arguing with Mave when she was hurt.

"Jody . . . ?" The voice was a croak. Jody spun around. Chael's eyes were open, and his lips moved as if he were laboring to speak again. Jody flew to the outlander, gripping the other's forearms as if he could anchor that wandering consciousness with his bare hands.

"Chael! Chael, can you hear me?"

Awareness of the here and now came slowly to Chael, as his mind returned from velvet fields ringed by stars and sweeping plains lying at the foot of ice cliffs. The whole universe seemed to slip away from him, leaving him anchored to only this one small point where his body rested.

"Water," he croaked and heard Jody run to fetch some. His eyes refused to focus, but his thoughts ran with unaccustomed clarity. The traders were doomed. Entrepreneurs, they made their living on the frontier. They dealt with the smaller, more primitive worlds and acted as go-betweens. But soon the Dann would control it all, for they controlled Ozine Station, the key to the wands. With stim and with plenty of prisoners to experiment on, the Dann would soon learn how to use that key. Right now, they didn't know what they held.

"Chael, think of a way out of here. Think of a way out!" Jody commanded, shaking him roughly. He felt a cup pressed to his lips and drank eagerly.

Yes, a way out for the traders; they need a strong ally. Slipping away from his body again, he viewed the matrix. All time and space spread out around him; up-time and down-time, near and far. his own present was the clearest, sharpest. Further away, the images became misty and harder to discern. Ozine Station shone like a beacon, brightly illuminated by the abundance of stim-awakened minds. Down-time, he saw the flickering glimmer of Mave's experiment. Another light caught his eye, a dim, yellow glow some distance away in space, but on the same plane in time.

Of course, here was the ally, the means of salvation for the traders and Ozine alike. Satisfied, he returned to his present surroundings. Jody, quietly despairing, had released him and sat next to his sister on the bunk. Chael knew the boy was trying to plan an escape. He also knew they'd all be killed if he didn't intervene. It wouldn't do. The traders were necessary to the future.

Mave lay with her eyes closed, her breathing fast and shallow. She should stay here, warm and quiet, but the Dann would come for them soon. But it was already too late. The door slid aside.

"Outside," the guard ordered. He gestured towards Mave. "Bring her along."

Jody picked her up in his arms like a child. Chael rose stiffly, and they marched back through the traders' sector. The bright walls were marred with blaster burns. Chael felt anger bubbling in him, but he held it back, tamped it down, saving that destructive energy for the moment when it could do them the most good. They halted at last before the entrance to one of the sleeping rooms, he didn't know whose.

"In there," the guard ordered, gesturing with a hand that ended in four long, ropy tentacles. One tentacle pressed the entry button, and the door slid aside.

The Dann captain faced them, lounging confidently on a delicately carved couch. He smiled, showing pointed yellow teeth.

"Come in. Be seated," Henyab said, gesturing expansively with one set of arms. The other two held blasters. Jody lowered his sister to a matching couch opposite the Dann, and Chael sat on a bench nearby. It was only then that he looked closely at the figure seated in the shadows near the captain.

"Lissa!" he blurted.

The Dann captain laughed. "You're surprised, eh?"

But Chael had control of himself again and rapidly calculated their chances. Henyab might have four arms, but he had only one pair of eyes. If they hit him from opposite directions . . . . There was no way to communicate with Lissa. After that first start at hearing her name, she sat as still as if carved from marble. He had to take a chance and hope she'd understand. The longer they waited, the worse off they'd be. Then Mave moaned, giving him an opening.

Briefly, the Dann's eyes flickered to where she lay on the couch. Chael moved up and forward in one fluid motion, throwing the bench he'd been sitting on and following it with a kick that started at ground level and ended against the Dann captain's head. Henyab was out cold before Chael's feet touched the ground. He crouched for a moment, wary, but the Dann didn't move.

Lissa was on her feet, looking so incredulous that Chael felt a momentary wave of irritation. Did she really think he could be led around so tamely?

"We've got to get out of here," Jody urged. Painfully, Mave sat up and, with her brother's help, made it to her feet.

"The storage bays," she said. "Our starships are there . . . ." Her voice ran down, and she leaned heavily against Jody.

"Let's go," Chael said, picking up the captain's blasters. He handed one to Jody. Chael took aim at the unconscious Dann, then stopped, unable to pull the trigger. To kill a man in war was one thing, but he was no coldblooded assassin. The Dann groaned.

"Kill him!" Lissa urged.

"No. Let's get out of here," Chael said.

"But the Dann ships will shoot us down," she protested. "Where can we go?"

"Anywhere," Chael said, grabbing her arm and dragging her along. "Just so it's away from here."

"No. I won't go." She tried to tug her arm free.

Chael shifted his grip on the blaster. This was no time to argue the merits of escape. He clipped her once, just above the temple. She folded, suddenly limp, and he threw her over his shoulder and hurried after the traders.

"Quick," Jody said. "In here." He thumbed open the storage bay doors, and they slipped inside. The bay was a huge, hollow chamber, lighted only intermittently by small light cubes. The trader starships looked like crouching birds in the twilight. Chael headed for the nearest one. They had only minutes before their escape was discovered. Jody helped Mave up the hatchway, while Chael carried Lissa. The boy strapped them in as Chael studied the controls. They were in a tiny, Class-C scout, the smallest, fastest ship in the bay. Chael hoped it would be fast enough to outrun the Dann fighters.

"Ready?" he asked.

"Ready," Jody affirmed, taking the co-pilot's seat.

Chael started the engines. The ship rose gracefully and sailed towards the double force-screen airlock. He keyed in the correct response, and the screens let them through. Once outside, he put the norm-space engines on full thrust to give them as much of a head start as possible. Jody was busy feeding their coordinates into the navigation computer.

"Where to?" the boy asked.

"Anywhere," Chael answered. The Dann had just

noticed them. Three fighters peeled off and picked up their wake.

"I'm setting course for Kovarall. It's the nearest civilized planet," Jody said.

Chael was too busy trying evasive maneuvers to reply. The little scout carried laser cannons, but he couldn't afford to let the Dann get close enough for him to use them. The Dann fighters had the range on their weapons.

"Almost ready," Jody said.

"Switch to light speed!" Chael ordered. The Dann fighters were almost on them. The ship shuddered as her light shielding took the first blasts. Then Jody threw the switch, and they sped into the faster-than-light dimension of hyperspace.

"We made it!" Jody yelled. But Chael was silent. Already, the stim was wearing off. He could feel the rapidly increasing pace of the decline in his own body. They had to land soon.

"Chael, what's wrong?" Jody asked anxiously.

"Can you bring this ship in by yourself?" Chael asked.

"Of course," Jody assured him. Just then the warning buzzer went off.

"We're losing power," Jody said after a rapid glance at the screens. "We've been hit. We're not going to make it to Kovarall. We'll have to set down now, where ever we are."

But Chael wasn't listening. With an animal growl, he lapsed into the dark phase of stim withdrawal.

Confusion, disorientation; he was too hot. Enclosed in some thick fur, he heard snatches of argument over his head.

" . . . will not! This is deception."

" . . . leader in our time of need . . . ."

"The Hawk people will kill him."

" . . . no matter."

"Hush, he's awake."

Eyes open, Chael examined the two women. One was slender, dark-haired, dressed only in a wolfskin cape, the black fur blending with her long, midnight hair. The skull fit over her own head like a helmet, and fangs gleamed on her forehead. Her hairless ivory skin was covered by neither shoes, sandals, nor shirt. She looked utterly self-possessed. The other woman was in total contrast in dress, but she had the same self-confident manner. Her hair was lighter—more a dark grey, although it didn't seem a sign of age—but she wore it pulled and plaited into an elaborate coiffure. Her dress was a long, white skin tunic, reaching from her shoulders to her ankles. She wore a necklace of white claws that made a clinking sound when she moved.

"Are you through with your assessment?" she asked coldly.

"Leave him be," said the one in the wolf fur. "He must rest and grow strong again."

The woman in white smiled mockingly. "Perhaps, sister, and perhaps he won't agree with your reading of his destiny." She turned and left, accompanied by the clink of fangs.

Warily, Chael watched the Wolf-witch. She seemed connected somehow with his dream-like memories of visions under stim, but they were fading rapidly. Almost automatically, he said, "My name is Chael."

The woman looked at him wide-eyed for a moment. "Then you will help! I knew you would!" she exclaimed. "My name is Ona, Priestess to the Wolf, Chael War Leader."

"Wait," said Chael. He felt he was being rushed

into something he wasn't sure he wanted to do. "I don't know what you're talking about."

"It doesn't matter," Ona interrupted imperiously. "You are here. You've come to save us, even if that idiot Balvar won't listen. You're being here is what matters." She was enthusiastic, electric, and maddeningly evasive. Chael felt overwhelmed. His impulse was to dig in and stubbornly refuse to go along with her careless plans for his destiny, but he had other questions he wanted answered, so he bridled his tongue. "Where are the people who were with me?" he asked. The vague unease he'd been feeling settled into a strong need to know the present whereabouts and health of the three traders.

"The women and the boy?" Ona said carelessly. "They're somewhere about the village. They aren't important. The Hawk people move deeper into our territory every day, but now you have come to drive them out. I have read it in the ashes and on the water. They will die in fire and burning. You will drive them out . . . ."

"Not alone," Chael interrupted. He didn't like her casual disregard of the traders, nor her quick assumption of control. This place looked as primitive as a Coss camp; the woman's barbaric clothes, the rude hut he was in, the fur bedclothes, all were far from the technological society he'd just left. The traders, however brave and competent, just weren't equipped to survive in such company.

"The Wolf people will help you," Ona said. "I shall tell them it is my will."

Chael was doubtful about just how readily the Wolf people would obey Ona's will. If that woman in white was anything to go by . . . .

"I need more than your people," Chael said firmly, deciding to play along. "The ones who came with me, they're my advisors. I can't fight without their help."

Ona frowned, and for a moment Chael wondered if he'd thrown away all their lives. He should have waited, learned the ground first, but it was always his way to move on instinct.

"Very well," Ona said crossly. "Although I can't see why you want them. They're too useless to even feed themselves."

"They've gone hungry?" Chael asked. He wondered suddenly just how long he'd been unconscious. Was Lissa all right?

"My fool of a sister has fed them," Ona said. "Kemmet thinks she can use them against me somehow. But she can't," Ona concluded harshly. The wolf skull gave her a ferocious look. "I have foreseen it. The Wolf shall eat up the Hawk."

Oddly, it was then that Chael noticed for the first time how young Ona was, younger even than Jody. She was slender and slightly built, reminding him of Sinshee, but Ona had a vibrant emotion and fire of life that the Ozine lacked.

"Battles aren't won without planning," Chael said. "Bring me my advisors."

"You dare give me orders!"

"You asked for a War Leader, not a servant," Chael said. He was determined to play his assigned role for all it was worth. Since he'd committed himself, he intended to get the upper hand with Ona now, while he still had a chance.

Silently, the Wolf-witch got up and left the hut. Chael hoped she was going to do his bidding, and not to bring the executioners. Too warm, he pushed back the furs covering him. He was naked, and the air was chill and damp. After a short search, he discovered his clothes in a small chest. He felt more comfortable when he was dressed.

Ona wasn't gone long. "Here they are," she announced, dramatically throwing back the flap of hide that served as a door. Mave and Lissa entered, trailed by Jody. They were dirty. Mave's arm was in a sling, and her face was gaunt. Lissa looked in better shape, Chael was relieved to see. Jody grinned at him. Arms folded across her chest, Ona stood by the door, making no move to leave.

"I want to talk to them alone," Chael announced, in what he hoped were properly firm tones.

"It is my will to stay with you," Ona countered.

"It is my will to be alone with my advisors," Chael insisted, falling into Ona's speech pattern. "Am I not the War Leader? Will you defeat the Hawk people alone?"

Angrily, Ona whirled and stamped out. Chael was sure that if a hide flap door could be slammed, his ears would be ringing.

"War Leader or witch baiter, you seem determined to lead a short life," Mave observed, sitting at the foot of his bed. She looked tired and drawn, but at least she could now walk without requiring Jody's support.

"We've got to get out of here!" Lissa declared impatiently.

"All in good time," Mave said. She sighed and leaned back against the sod wall.

"Just let me know what's going on," Chael asked. "All I know is that I woke up with Ona and her sister having a fight over my head. From what they let slip, things haven't been going well for you three."

"We've had some problems," Mave admitted, smiling slightly.

"Some problems!" Lissa said. "First, they were going to kill us with those ridiculous spears, then they decided to let us starve. If Kemmet hadn't taken us in, we'd be dead by now.'' She paused to glare at Jody. ''I don't know what you were thinking of, setting us down on this barbarian dump.''

''There wasn't any choice,'' Jody said patiently. It was obviously an old argument. He turned to Chael. ''We lost our hyperdrive engines. According to the charts, this was the nearest planet with any kind of civilized communications equipment. There's a small outpost north of here.

''We came down in the lifeboat. It landed about a kilometer from here on ground the spring rains had turned into a swamp. We lost the lifeboat, the emergency gear, our blasters—everything. We were lucky to get out alive. We're a long way from the outpost, but we've still got a chance.''

''The barbarians did want to leave us for the wolves at first, but Kemmet sorted that out pretty fast. Her motto is: whatever's bad for Ona is good for Kemmet.''

''And vice versa,'' Mave added. ''Kemmet is married to the local chief. She sees Ona's power as a threat to her own.''

''A nice mess,'' Chael said gloomily. ''Maybe I should have kept silent.''

''Well, Kemmet didn't look happy when Ona sailed in saying you were the War Leader and asking for your staff,'' Jody said. ''You really intend to go along with this?''

''It looks like it, unless I can think of a way out fast.''

''Well,'' Jody said thoughtfully. ''I did get a reading on the outpost. If we can get provisions and something warm to wear, we could make it there and use the com-link. But it won't be easy. This world is in the middle of an ice age. I saw glaciers over three-quarters of the land mass before we landed. If the

56

inhabitants are all as barbaric as these Wolf people, we could have some problems."

"I think it's remarkable that you're alive at all," Mave said. "That was quite an overdose you took."

Chael grunted. He remembered what had happened to the second experimenter. At least there wouldn't be any stim for him to steal here.

Lissa sat down at his other side. She placed a soft hand on his good arm. "I'm sure you'll think of a way out, Chael," she said, her earlier bad temper forgotten. He slipped an arm around her waist, but no useful ideas came to him.

"We have to hope the Dann are holding my Household for hostages," Mave said. "The League has many Dann prisoners—maybe an exchange." She drew herself up with visible effort. They all knew the Household's chances of survival were slim.

"In the meantime, we must find a way to the outpost and that, I'm afraid, means overcoming Ona's Hawk people."

The next hour's discussion of ways and means left Chael more discouraged than ever. He was no War Leader, not that the great battle between the Wolf and the Hawk would count as more than a skirmish on Fenmark. But he'd always been more used to taking orders than giving them. Fenmark had no use for an outlander officer. He considered the facts. There were maybe fifty fighters on each side, if Mave's information were correct, all able-bodied adults without children.

Maternal responsibilities among their barbarian hosts followed no division by sex, age, or any other pattern that Mave had been able to determine. Some raised children, some didn't, but the number of parents generally came to about one-third of the adult population, an adult being anyone who had gone through the rite of passage. Even that wasn't strictly necessary, but it was considered a solecism of no mean order to remain a child after the age of twenty-five or so. Ona, naturally, had gone through the rite as early as possible. He might like Ona, Chael reflected, if only she weren't so domineering.

The Wolf-witch had had someone wash his clothes, and they were still clammy-damp as he dressed for the evening ceremony. Time was running out. The short spring day was nearly over, and tonight the Wolf people would gather in their chief's house for the spring rite of passage and a discussion of the coming war. This was Chael's chance to view his troops. Full of doubts, he awaited Ona's summons.

6

Chael felt even more uneasy as he marched a step behind Ona into the oversized sod cabin that served as the chief's house and town hall. Mave and Jody were right behind him. Lissa, for reasons of her own, had elected to stay away. He forced himself to walk proudly, knowing that neither of the traders would be slouching. Ona took the path down the center of the room, and Chael was conscious of the assembled barbarians watching them; some interested, some hostile, most simply wary. He followed Ona up to a bench that ran across the front of the room. When she turned and sat without ceremony, Chael and his companions did the same.

There were no cries of outrage, and no spears thudded in their direction. He glanced curiously over the assembly. The Wolf people were small and slender, but they tended to a wiry, sinewy strength. He judged them tougher than he'd thought. Male and female, they carried the strong, ropy muscles of barbarians used to hard labor and deprivation. He'd back them against a similarly-sized, similarly-armed group of Dann any day. They all carried spears tipped with chipped stone points and had stone knives at their belts. But the Hawk people, chael felt sure, would be just the same. How could he deliberately lead these people into mutual annihilation, or at best, a standoff that would cost both tribes more than they could afford in people and resources?

Another man had entered the hall, the chief Balvar, Chael supposed. Kemmet walked half a step behind him, but it was plain who really ran things. Balvar, old, burly, and battle-scarred, was no match for his intelligent, ambitious wife, or for his sister-in-law, Chael thought glancing sideways at Ona. Ona stared straight ahead, seeming oblivious to Balvar, to Kemmet, to the whole noisy crowd pounding the butts of their spears against the dirt floor in approval of their chief. Balvar and his entourage took their places in the center of the long, curved bench, and Chael had a clear view of them.

"What now?" he whispered.

"Passage rites," Jody answered out of the side of his mouth. "Or so Ona said."

"Silence!" the wolf-witch hissed.

Intent on learning as much as he could, Chael watched the show unfolding in the clear space between the bench and the spectators seated on the floor. Three youths dressed in white loincloths entered from the back of the room. Their bodies were painted in abstract, elongated red and black designs. They came in quietly and sat cross-legged on the floor, facing Balvar.

Chael glanced at Ona, expecting her to take part in this ritual, but she made no move to rise. No one, in fact, moved, and Chael began to feel restless. The bench was hard, his legs were cramped, and there was an unpleasant itch in the middle of his back. He repressed a yawn between clenched teeth. Well, he'd been far more uncomfortable on many a night watch.

The yowling scream that followed nearly caused him to leap from the bench. Only Jody's arm put out in quick restraint kept him from leaping to his feet in instant battle readiness. A figure followed the voice; impossible to tell whether it was male or female. Particolored furs and feathers covered the torso in a loose cloak. The arms and legs were painted red, and on the head—a mask? The silvery globe had no apparent seam or joint in its mirror-like surface. In any case, a people using tools of stone and bone shouldn't have the technology to make anything like that polished helmet.

"Trade goods?" Chael whispered.

"I've never seen anything like it," Mave replied softly.

Now the helmeted figure began to dance and chant around the three seated initiates. But how does he see? Chael wondered. There were no openings in the helmet, no eyeholes, nor even an opening to breathe through. It was as if there were a round, gleaming ball where the head should be, and the metal merged smoothly, imperceptibly, into the skin of the neck. The thing was beautiful, seemingly simple, yet utterly complex. Abruptly, the chanting stopped. The shaman stood facing Balvar, arms outspread. The silence seemed thick, menacing to Chael. Then, prosaically enough, Balvar spoke.

"Tonight is the time of passage," he said, obviously repeating a well-worn formula. "Are all the children present for their last night?" He looked around the audience, but no one stirred. The three initiates stared blankly downwards.

"So be it," Balvar said. "Let the . . . what?" The last was a startled grunt. Kemmet had punched him sharply in the ribs with her elbow. So Balvar had fluffed his lines, Chael thought. The chief gathered his dignity around him and glared at the assembly, as if daring anyone to notice the incident.

"Ah, there is a question about the proposed War Leader," Balvar began hesitantly. With a sinking feeling, Chael thought he knew what was coming. Impatiently, Kemmet took over.

"We need to know whether this 'War Leader,' " the words dripped skepticism, "is in fact a war leader. Is this person even an adult?"

Beside him, Chael felt Ona quivering. It was like sitting next to a dynamo. The hairs on the nape of his neck rose, and his scalp prickled. His hand, went automatically to where his blaster should be, but met empty air. Ona stood, and Chael was surprised at how controlled she was. The witch girl was proving more formidable than he'd thought.

"Kemmet, you go too far!" Her voice was full of warning, but Kemmet was confident of her own power.

"You expect us to trust our lives to a stranger? Let the stranger prove himself first."

"He was sent by the Wolf!"

"Was he?" Kemmet smiled bitterly. "Perhaps my

sister, in her innocence, forgets that there are other powers than the Wolf.''

''Not so!'' Ona said hotly.

Keep calm, Ona, Chael thought. Balvar interrupted at this point. Perhaps out of a need to assert his damaged authority, he decided to settle matters himself.

''We will have a vote,'' he commanded.

''A vote! A vote!'' shouted the assembled warriors.

Ona scowled, and Kemmet looked equally displeased, but it was too late to change anything now.

''Shall the stranger take the test?'' Balvar asked.

''Yes!'' The call was unanimous, emphasized by the pounding of spearbutts against the floor. Chael heard it with fatalistic acceptance. It seemed his destiny to fall from one disaster to another, most of them precipitated by his own actions. All he wanted was to be free—to go where he pleased when he pleased to do it. It wasn't even a very ambitious dream. It was just impossible.

Calmly, he walked past the seething Ona, away from the worried traders, and sat cross-legged with the other initiates. He scarcely noticed when the shaman's chant began again. Chael was at the end of the line, and the masked figure began the rite with the ''child'' farthest from him. The masked one handed each in turn a small wad of leaves, then moved back to the other end of the line. Chael started slightly, jarred out of his apathy. The leaves were stim, raw, unprocessed. He'd been sensitized. He couldn't mistake stim, even in this unfamiliar form; his body knew. Ideas snapped together like relays closing in his mind, and he knew where he was: Ozine Home!

He was about to undergo an alien rite designed for an alien people. If he lived through that, he'd be lucky beyond belief, and even so, he'd still have more problems than he cared to face. The only way to survive was to take it all moment by moment, and hope that somehow this knowledge could help him win his freedom.

He noticed the other initiates putting the wads of raw stim leaves in their mouths. Unhesitatingly, he did the same. The shaman fell silent and sat on the floor facing them. For a long time, nothing seemed to happen. Chael didn't care. He was busy exploring the stim-enhanced sensation of nowness. The sight of the dimly lighted room with its rows of smoky torches; the close, subtly alien odor of Ozine bodies (the smell was easily identifiable now that he'd taken the stim); the heat, cut by chill drafts; the slightly acid taste of the stim leaves; all the sensations combined to make him intensely aware of where he was.

Gradually, there came to him an acute sense of danger. Then he noticed a slow movement in the boy seated next to him. The lithe, slender body leaned forward slowly from the waist, as if the muscles around the spine had melted their firm support. Soundlessly, the boy slumped over his still-crossed legs. Chael felt one of the loose arms brush his thigh. With a slight shock, he noticed that the Ozine had stopped breathing. Chael spread his stim-heightened awareness and felt the last quick flutters of the boy's heart. He was dead. Chael was puzzled. There was no mark, no violence; poison? he wondered. But whatever it was, it seemed to have no effect on him. Alert now, he strained his senses still further, searching for the danger. He was the watcher, waiting wide-awake in a still pool of self.

Gradually, he became aware of the other. His eyes turned involuntarily toward the mask. Outwardly, the polished ball merely reflected his own face, dark and distorted on the curved surface, but Chael thought he felt menace there, a creeping danger that waited the chance to destroy him. Cautiously, he probed with his mind. Equally cautious, the other withdrew. Chael felt a surge of triumph but held himself in check. The opponent was confident too. Slowly, like wrestlers circling one another on the mat, they drew together again. Chael was oblivious to everything but the other. The room, the assembly, Mave, Jody, Ona, even Lissa, all faded before the nearness of that presence. It was like an overpowering odor, paralyzing his other senses.

Suddenly, Chael tried a rapid thrust, jabbing against the other's defenses. He slammed full tilt into resistance like a wall and was flung back, stunned. Before he could recover, his opponent slashed him with a similar thrust. Chael gasped. The pain was physical, like a swift kick in the groin. He felt the blood leave his face. Furiously, he leaped at his opponent, sending blows of mental force that should have trampled the other under his wild anger, but none reached past that blank barrier. The return attack left him doubled over and gasping, a trickle of blood and drool running down his chin from where he'd bitten his lip.

He drew inward, shutting himself into a small, tight ball of being. He waited, braced, but there was no move from the other. He waited longer, but there was only the sense of alien self. Chael breathed freely again, and his heart slowed to a more normal speed. With only a part of his mind keeping cautious watch, he took time to think. The sense of otherness came from the shaman, he was sure of it. But what was happening? His life depended upon knowing. Action, reaction, he thought. Attack led to attack. Withdrawal led to withdrawal. So it was time to try something new. Very cautiously, Chael extended a tentacle of self. It was a small part of him, probing but not aggressive.

The probe met the barrier and passed effortlessly through. There was an other there, not the same as he'd seen from the outside. The outside was a mask, a reflection. Inside, there was warmth, friendship, acceptance. Chael felt himself enveloped in love. A sense of congratulations, of well-wishing, reached him. He'd passed the test. He was accepted. He knew he had an idiot grin on his face, and he felt the tears streaming out of his eyes. He didn't care. He was drunk on love, on belonging. He, Chael the outlander, belonged, however briefly. It was a gift he'd never give up.

Gradually, the other withdrew, and Chael found himself once more alone in his own head. It didn't matter. The good feeling remained. He looked with love at Ona, Kemmet, Balvar, and all the Wolf people. They were his people. The ceremony was over. The dead child was carried away. The new adults took their places among their peers. Chael felt only a passing regret for the dead boy. There were so many more who were alive to care for.

"Here, take him and keep him quiet," Ona told Jody roughly. "He'll be back to normal in the morning."

Gently, Jody guided him to a seat beside Mave. Chael subsided happily. All he wanted was to enjoy this wonderful new feeling of belonging.

"What's the matter with him?" Jody asked, sitting down. "I thought he was dying at first, now he looks like somebody's given him a jolt of happy juice."

"I don't know," Mave said, putting her arm around the outlander so he wouldn't fall from his seat. "I hope Ona's right, and his brain will unscramble tomorrow."

Jody looked worried but asked no more questions.

Ona was speaking again—a long, rhythmic speech about the Wolf devouring the Hawk—with the aid of the new War Leader and, of course, Ona herself.

7

Chael's euphoria was gone by the second day of their trek across the tundra. The boggy ground squelched and slurped at his new leggings. His uniform boots were too worn to be comfortable on Ozine Home, and he'd been glad to accept the warm, dry footwear when Ona offered it. Chael, Ona, Jody, and Lissa were now about three days march from their destination—or so the Wolf-witch said. Chael saw no landmarks on the flat, wet ground. The terrain was severe, with only occasional copses of stunted trees to mark the presence of springs. The hills were low and rolled imperceptibly into one another. Chael walked close to Lissa, but she ignored him, angry because this march was very much against her wishes. Chael had refused to leave her in Kemmet's care. It was bad enough that Mave was still too weak to come with them.

Chael was silent too, resentful of the rebuff. He couldn't understand Lissa; one moment she favored him and the next she didn't. Surely she hadn't really wanted to stay on Ozine Station, a prisoner of the Dann? He wanted to talk to her about his experience during the initiation and to tell her about his discovery:

this was Ozine Home! The knowledge was important, although he wasn't sure just now. But Lissa had no time for him, so he kept his news to himself.

They climbed a low bluff where run-off had cut channels in the soil. Eyes on the ground, Chael followed Ona up the hill. One careless step could sprain an ankle. He reached the top without mishap and looked down. The grass was like a miracle; rich, vibrant, the individual blades grew so close together that the plain resembled a dense, green fur. It was like nothing he'd ever seen. The scent was spicy and enticing.

"The Kor-grass," Ona said softly. For a moment, they stood drinking in the color and perfume. Then Ona shook herself and started off briskly at her steady, enduring pace.

"Come on," she said. "We've got a long way to go yet."

Chael's depression dispersed, washed away by the fresh wind blowing over the Kor-grass. He glanced at Jody and smiled. The boy grinned back.

"Over your hangover?" the young trader asked.

"You bet," Chael answered. So what if he wasn't really one of the Wolf people? In a way, he still belonged. That was as much as he wanted. He was free. Life was good. The contented mood stayed with him over the rest of the journey, despite the icy ooze that trickled through the roots of the Kor-grass, despite the fatigue and the chill, damp skins that were his bed at night. Not even Lissa's continued coldness lowered his spirits.

On the morning of the fifth day, they reached the Hawk people. They stopped at a distance and lay flat, hidden by the lush grass at the top of a long ridge. The Hawk camp was a handful of hide lean-tos dominated by the larger tent of the chief. Well, he hadn't expected anything better. In the background, Ona muttered in dark outrage.

"On our land! Thieves! Murderers!"

To Chael, there seemed to be more than enough land for all. The morning fog lifted, and the treeless horizon stretched on to a grey blur in the distance. He looked again at the horizon—ice, a wall of ice marking the ends of the earth. He shivered; so much water, so much cold, and all of it flowing inexorably towards them.

"How about moving in for a closer view?" Jody asked, bringing him down to earth.

"I don't like it," Lissa complained. "I don't think we should go any closer." Her eyes were blue slits of bad temper.

"We're here to scout," Chael said, edging forward on his belly. The rest followed—even Lissa, reluctantly. It took a long time to cross the next kilometer. Chael's shirt was glued to his back with sweat, yet his hands and belly were icy. The Kor-grass made him itch, and he wondered how Ona was doing, still attired only in her wolfskin cloak. Despite the Wolf-witch's indifference to the cold, Chael was sure she must be miserable.

They were closer to the camp now and further west. People wandered among the hide shelters. They wore furs and skins with necklaces of bone or teeth. Set them down among Ona's people, Chael thought, and he wouldn't be able to tell Hawk from Wolf. They moved about getting breakfast, yawning, stretching. No one behaved as though they considered themselves in enemy territory. A woman came out of one of the larger tents. Like Ona, she was dressed only in a dark cape. She spat, then bowed ceremoniously in four directions. That done, she picked up a small bag and began walking away from the camp—towards their hiding place.

"Be still," Ona whispered. "She hasn't seen us." She laid a restraining hand on Chael's arm. He subsided, watching the approaching Hawk-witch. He was sure that's what she must be, for her cape was made up of dark, irridescent feathers. A carved bird's head with a curved hunting beak formed a hood for the cloak. The woman was old, her body thin and sinewy. Her breasts hung in flat flaps that jiggled against her ribs. Her face was seamed, and her nose curved to match the Hawk beak above it. She looked very old, very wise. She passed within a few yards of where they lay hidden in the long grass. Chael looked down at the ground as she went by. He was afraid that she could feel his eyes on her as she passed. He watched a small, red bug struggling over the long stems. Abruptly, a black beatle darted out of the grass and swallowed the red bug whole. Chael looked away.

The Hawk-witch squatted in the grass only a short distance beyond their hiding place. Her back was to them, and all he could see was the blue-black sheen of her feathered hood. She hummed and clicked to herself, but if she were using any words, they didn't make sense to Chael. A dark, grey smoke rose from around the witch, and his nose twitched as he smelled the burning stim leaves. He rose slightly, wanting to be closer to the fire. Jody and Ona pinned him to the ground.

"Keep down, you fool!" Ona snarled.

"I'm getting away from here," Lissa said. She backed away from them, moving like some small animal in the grass.

"No, wait!" Jody said.

The grass parted, and a spear slammed into the ground a finger's breadth from Chael's nose. Slowly,

69

they looked up at the circle of their captors.

At least Lissa had escaped, Chael thought as he stared at the blank wall of their tent. He was cold, wet, dirty, and hungry. He'd been shot at, beaten, stabbed, dosed and overdosed with alien drugs. He was probably going to die messily in the morning.

His right foot was cramped, but he didn't want to move, because Jody and Ona were lying half on top of him and sound asleep. It was odd the way they'd taken to huddling together in the days since their capture. It wasn't so much for warmth as for comfort. It was important to have friends in the midst of so many enemies. Chael sighed and tried to ease his foot without waking them.

If he turned his head slightly, he could see out the flap of the tent—see a dark sky that drooped toward night and the impassive backs of their guards. The flap stirred, and the Hawk-witch entered. For a moment, she and Chael stared eye to eye. The witch's eyes were round, dark brown, and fierce.

"So," she said slowly, "they made no mistake. You are indeed an outlander."

"My home is far away from here," Chael conceded.

"You speak and yet you don't," the woman said. "Your words are not in our language."

"A machine brings my thoughts to you and yours to me," Chael told her. He was impressed by the witch's shrewdness. She was the only one on Ozine Home who'd noticed the translator, and noticed it as soon as he spoke.

"Where is this machine?" she asked.

Chael raised one hand to his temple. "Here," he said, "in my head." He hoped he was right. He really knew no more about the Ozine-made translator than

70

the Hawk-witch. The woman looked at him closely for a moment. Her nostrils flared as she sniffed deeply. She seemed to be testing the air for the smell of truth.

"The others with you, are they the same?"

"The boy is. He came with me. The woman is from this world." Then Chael found himself pouring out the whole strange story, his own longings, the wand, Ozine Station, the Dann, Mave and her Household. He didn't know if the woman understood what he told her. Blasters, cities, his very concepts of the Universe were probably alien to her, but Chael felt pressed by a need to talk. Too much had happened, and it was time to set the story straight. The Hawk-witch was wise. Her breasts were the flat flaps of an old woman, but her eyes were bright.

The witch sat very still for some time after he'd finished. The beak of her hood cast a shadow over her face, and her feathered cape draped around her. It was nearly dark. The spring twilight was ending. On his lap, Ona muttered in her sleep, then rolled over and was silent again.

"A strange tale, outlander. Yet I think it true. We have our legends; they may be true, too."

"All we want," Chael said, "is to reach the outpost and return to our own people."

"I've heard of such an outpost, far north of here," the witch said. "But that was when I was only a girl. There's been no word for many summers. The ice may have swallowed it."

Chael's heart sank. It made no difference to him whether he stayed here or returned to Ozine Station, either place was a trap; but he feared for Mave and her Household. Time was growing short. They'd already been on Ozine Home almost a month. Time didn't run at the same rate everywhere, or so he'd been taught, but it was surely passing for the Household as well as for them. He only hoped that the clock hadn't already run out for the traders left with the Dann.

"We just want to go our way," Chael repeated.

"Yet, you are the War Leader." She didn't explain how she knew.

"I'd rather lead them away from war," Chael answered honestly. "There's plenty of land."

"The Wolf people are afraid that they will lose it all; that between us and the ice, there will be nothing left for them. That is not what I want," she said, emphasizing the 'I.' There was a thoughtful silence between them.

"We could be allies, you and I," she said.

"We could."

The witch drew a deep breath, then committed herself. "My name is Tsada."

"My name is Chael," he answered, marveling at the persistence of Ozine customs across time and space. How many generations ago had Katt and Sinshee's ancestors left this world? And now he had an ally.

But at dawn he felt less confident. Their hands bound behind their backs, they were led out into the small clearing near the camp. The mist still covered the plains, and the camp seemed sealed off from the world. Chael felt huge and awkward; even the brawniest of his Ozine captors was only half his size. He was a head taller than any of the Hawk people. Slowly, the clan gathered around them.

"What are they up to?" Jody asked.

"A hunt," Ona said, and her voice trembled. It was the first time they'd seen her afraid. She strained futilely at the ropes that held her wrists.

"What do you mean?" asked Jody. He moved

closer, as if trying to comfort her. But there was no time for explanation. Flanked by an honor guard of six spearbearers, Tsada approached them. Ignoring the prisoners, she spat once, bowed to the four directions and began the strange clicking chant Chael had first heard her use just before they were captured.

The sound irritated him. It was like listening to something just a little too far away to understood, like a dialogue in another room. The sounds were there, almost making sense, but their meaning continually eluded him. Tsada seemed to speak of woods, wild animals, a race of people who traveled on and on through time in endless generations. There was weight and repetition in what she said. Her chant embodied the millenia. The chant rose, wailing for what was lost and finally swearing to protect what remained. Abruptly, it was over.

Chael was disturbed by the sense of defiance and of time, by the force of the past. He shook off the hypnosis. Something new occurred. There was a stir at the back of the crowd, and the people parted, still silent. A woman appeared, pulling a small cage on wheels behind her. It was just large enough for one person to stand upright in, for two if they crowded, but no occupant would be able to move more than half a step in any direction. The woman stopped in the middle of the plaza, and Chael resolved to die before he'd enter the cage.

"We are the hunters," Tsada said. "Let the hunt begin." Her guard produced a small, wriggling animal, its brown and white fur matted with mud. It was about the size of a cat and whimpered pitifully, as if guessing its fate. Tsada raised a wooden knife, its blade fire-hardened and curved in a sickle shape. It looked as deadly as the great beak it was supposed to represent.

At a nod from the Hawk witch, two of the guards flipped the whimpering sacrifice over onto its back and held it there. Tsada raised the knife high, then plunged it down into the victim's belly. Red blood stained the dirty fur, and Chael thought his ears would be pierced by the high whistle of the death cry. The animal twisted once in agony, then, mercifully, was still. Chael let out a long sigh. The smell of blood was cloying. Would it be their turn next? He saw Jody standing stiff and watchful, and his own eyes narrowed in calculation as he waited for the next move. Ona had gone pale. She seemed overcome by an unnatural, fatalistic calm. Tsada plunged her hands into the bloody cavity and pulled out the still warm intestines. She held them close to examine them. Meanwhile, the guards cut the bonds at the prisoners' wrists.

"The stranger!" Tsada cried. Whirling, she flung the bloody mess at Chael. Violently, he knocked it away from him and crouched, waiting for the attack, but none came. The Ozine backed away, giving him a wide berth. Tense silence followed.

"The game is chosen," Tsada said. A murmur arose. Chael backed away. Tsada's honor guard closed in on Jody and Ona, herding them into the cage. They were hoisted high overhead on the scaffold.

"You will have until the torch burns out before the hunt begins," Tsada said. She looked at Chael and seemed to be trying to convey some hidden meaning. "If you elude the hunt, you will live. If you free your friends, they will live too. Otherwise, they remain in the cage until they die." Chael saw one of the warriors hand up a small skin bag of water and another of food. It was enough for about three days. Chael looked at Tsada again. He was caught up in alien customs once more. Hesitantly, he stepped back. The Ozine behind him moved out of his way. No one looked at him.

They all stared at the flaming torch.

"Run, Chael!" Ona ordered.

He took to his heels.

8

The ravine dropped steep and sheer for thirty meters. Doggedly, Chael followed the wandering path of the narrow stream. He had no plan, other than to run. The Hawk hunters would track him down if he tried to rest, and there was no place to hide. The tiny stream spread out, and he splashed in ice water to his ankles.

The cave was just a darker shadow when he first spotted it. But for the bird-thing that sprang away with a startled flutter of feathers, he would never have noticed the small, triangular opening. Recklessly, he crawled in, and there were no inhabitants to dispute his possession. It felt good to be out of the wind. He tucked his chilled hand under the front of his tunic to warm it and peered outside. There was no one in sight, but he must move on soon. The hunters wouldn't be far behind. But first, he'd rest for just a moment.

Mave lay on the bed of furs. She was weak, but the bout of fever had ended. She longed fiercely for the others to return, to be on her way back to her Household. Anxiety for them gnawed at her and refused to let her rest. The Dann had become alien during their long mutation—no matter that their ancestors were human—and she couldn't predict their actions. She only hoped the outlander Chael could end this barbarian war soon. In the meantime, she had to be ready to move quickly when the chance came. She turned to the bowl of stew Kemmet's servant had left for her. The smell made her gag, but she had to eat to regain her strength. Resolutely, she forced down a mouthful, but the sudden clamor outside made her drop her spoon.

Staggering a little, she reached the doorway. She leaned against the frame as she pulled aside the flap that covered the entrance. Lissa stood in the center of a group of excited Wolf people. She had returned—alone.

Thunder crashed, and Chael sat up with a jerk. Blinking, he hastily scanned the cave. No change. The thunder sounded again, and rain poured down outside. He must have fallen asleep, despite his intentions. Well, he decided, it was better this way. The rain would wash out his trail and slow his pursuers. In the meantime, he had a dry place to shelter in. He was worried about Jody and Ona in the exposed cage, but there was nothing he could do, not now. One glance outside convinced him of the inadvisability of proceding through the storm on foot. The meandering stream was now a torrent, and mud from the banks fell into it in chunks. His shelter was high enough to be safe—he hoped. He was hungry and thirsty; the hunger he must endure, but the thirst . . . .

His cupped hands held little, but the water poured down fast enough to allow Chael to drink his fill in just a few minutes. Then he settled back against the cave wall, trying to make himself comfortable until the rain stopped. Changes were coming too fast. He needed time to think, to try to get things in order. He was tired of reacting blindly to one event after another.

Why had Tsada chosen him as the quarry? He was sure she'd faked the divination. That meant she wanted him free for purposes of her own. True, she'd exchanged names with him. That linked them in some Ozine way that he didn't fully understand, but it wasn't the same as a knife oath. Well, he thought, rubbing a frayed patch on the knee of his uniform trousers, suppose they ousted the Dann from Ozine Station, never mind all the difficulties in the way, what then? He had to get a ship. The wand was out of the question, he finally admitted, but surely he could get a ship somehow. If he could just earn his passage out, he could get work as a hand on a freighter. The interior worlds of the League were almost totally mechanized, but out on the Rim, human muscle was still the cheapest source of labor. The Rim was wide open. Anything could happen there.

The shuffle of footsteps outside the cave interrupted his heady dreams. The rain had diminished, falling now in a fine drizzle. Thunder sounded, far-off and muted. It wasn't loud enough to drown out the soft snuffling outside. Chael sat very still. He had small hope of being overlooked. Feet squelched in the mud, and he heard a deep snort. Puzzled, he edged towards the cave mouth. A wall of grey hide moved past the opening, and he choked on the rank odor of animal—a big, big animal. The ground shook as it passed.

Instinctively, Chael pressed prone against the muddy floor. He knew it was a cavi. There was no mistaking that huge, battleship form. Ona had pointed out a herd grazing in the distance during their march to the Hawk camp. Not that the beast was a meat eater—cavii favored the Kor-grass—but it would probably kill him before deciding that he wasn't palatable.

He looked up and saw an enormous golden eye looking back at him. It filled the entrance. The red veins that wandered over the white were as thick as his thumb. The slit pupil ran vertically for the length of his arm. Looking into it was like peering into eternity. The eye blinked once. Skin like grey armour slid down over it, then lifted. Abruptly, it was withdrawn, and Chael breathed a sigh of relief.

But the relief was premature. The tip of a pale pink tongue began edging into the cave. Chael backed as far away as he could, but the cave soon narrowed into a dark burrow too small for him to enter. Reaching behind him, he felt a bundle of branches and debris blocking the way. The pink tongue quested after him. He eluded it and tugged at the nest. The odor of dust and rotten wood, the stink of the cavi's breath, and the reek of his own sweaty desparation were overpowering. Dizzy and nauseated, he gave a final desperate pull. The plug came away with a jerk. He staggered a step foward and fell against the tongue. It gave with a muscular resiliency, writhing under him. He threw himself back, landing beside the rotted mass of nest materials.

He shoved it at the searching tongue and threw himself into the dark opening he'd unclogged. The tunnel went back a dozen steps, then the moist dirt slipped and crumbled beneath him. He staggered back, but the whole mass broke away and went speeding down the steep incline with Chael on top of it.

"They're dead," Lissa said quietly, "all of them."

"Are you sure?" Mave asked. If she had even one small hope . . . .

"I saw them die," Lissa said firmly. "It was all over within a few hours after they were captured."

Mave turned away, unwilling to let the other woman

see her grief. Lissa looked after her—and smiled.

The slide seemed to go on forever. The tunnel twisted and curved sickeningly in absolute darkness. Then, gradually, the slope decreased, and Chael's wild ride slowed and finally came to a halt. The matted debris below him was hot to the touch from the friction of the slide, but Chael was unhurt. He lay still for a long moment, stunned. Slowly, his sense of purpose returned. Black despair hovered at the edge of consciousness, but he'd been close to death too many times to give in so easily. It had given him a fatalistic belief in his own destiny; it wasn't time to die yet.

His long fall had dropped into a dark, cylindrical tunnel. The air was dank and the footing slippery. To his left was utter blackness. The chute he'd slid down was impossible to climb, he discovered after a number of futile tries, but far ahead there was a dim blue light. Doggedly, he headed for it. The tunnel was warm compared to the air outside, and he was soon sweating heavily. He paused to take off his tunic, tying the sleeves around his waist. The gold navigator's medallion bumped against his chest. He felt stronger just knowing it was there. He had a reason to live, a prize to win.

Soon, he was close enough to see the rent the blue light entered through. It spilled across his path, showing the man-high pipe for what it was. Once, there had been a grill here, but it had long since fallen and lay in rusting flakes about the opening. Chael stepped through and quickly skipped to one side. He was alert, ready.

The plaza stretched before him, so enormous that it took several moments for his brain to make sense of what he was seeing. Pillar fled from pillar, and aisles rolled like highways. Tier upon tier of walkways rose, circled, and vanished into the twilight. Somber blues and purples, brilliant pink, yellow, red, and green repeated over and over in a bewildering pattern of color. Confused, dazed, Chael felt himself drawn through the fast-moving structure of color, line, and form. There was so much life, movement, purpose!

But nothing moved. The dead silence mocked the illusion of life. The stunning impact passed and in a few seconds, the awesome became familiar. The mundane obtruded itself. He noticed the thick dust on the floor, the patches of mould staining the magnificent colors. There were dark areas where the ancient lights had failed. So this was how the Ozine had once lived, he thought in awe.

But he couldn't stay here, to add his bones to the monument. The shaman who tested the Wolf children wore a helmet that must have come from such a place as this. The precipitous chute he'd fallen down couldn't be used as an easy entrance, but perhaps there were other, more accessible openings on the outside world. The entrance to an ascending ramp rested in the shadows a quarter of a kilometer away, and Chael strode towards it.

The gloom grew thicker near the ramp entrance. Most of the lights were out for the height of a full two stories above his head. Soft beams filtered down from the lofty regions above, but they were soon diffused by the lacework of catwalks and pillars. The remaining low level lights only served to confuse his vision as his eyes tried vainly to adjust to the rapid changes from light to dark and dark to light. So Chael's toes actually hung over the edge of the pit before he saw it. He backstepped hastily in a kind of skittering hop, his heart thudding from the burst of adrenalin.

Cautiously, he approached the abyss. It was a trench, wider than he could leap and too deep for him to see the bottom. It ran like a great scar on the face of the city, and either end vanished into infinity. He knelt at the edge, examining the smooth walls. The gash was lined with black, powdery ash. He rubbed some between his fingers, puzzled by its fine, silty texture. Gradually, he realized what he rested by. It was a burn scar, like the scars made by a blaster, but larger, much larger. He felt horror as he imagined how the monstrous beam must have lashed the city like a whip. This was far different from honorable hand-to-hand combat. Abruptly, Chael rose and dusted his hands against his pants. The trough barred his way to the ramp. He would seek another exit.

He followed the edge of the trough, hoping he'd soon find a clear path to one of the ramps that rose at intervals along the perimeter of the plaza. The lights shifted and flickered, so that the shadows changed constantly. Chael found himself looking over his shoulder and starting at the sudden changes in light. He forced himself to be calm, but the dead city oppressed him.

At last, the scar ended and there, just beyond it, was another ramp. Chael hurried towards it. His footsteps stirred a flurry of fine dust and made him sneeze so that his eyes watered, and he stumbled into something that crunched like dry sticks. When the dust subsided, he bent to look at his find. A delicate skull lay face up on the floor. There were still strands of long, dark hair clinging to it, and a gold chain gleamed among the vertebrae of the neck. He'd stepped on an arm. The ulna lay in splinters. The bones seemed child-sized—Ozine bones.

Slowly, he rose and dusted his hands, then continued on towards the ramp. The number of ancient skeletons increased as he neared the base of the ramp until, at last, he walked through brittle bones and rags that sometimes reached above his knees. The dead Ozine lay piled on one another, haphazardly, choking the ramp. Chael imagined the panicked rush as they fled from the burning white beam, the scramble for the ramp, the wild stampede over the bodies of the fallen—it was all written clearly in the mounds and heaps of the dead. Grimly, he marched through the bones. He refused to feel.

At about the third level, the ramp cleared, and he walked more freely. There was more light here, too. He seemed to be in a shopping arcade. The drop to the plaza below was at his right hand, but to his left, shop windows shone as brightly as if the customers were expected back at any moment. Other windows were dark, and he didn't venture too close to their cavernous mouths. Here and there, lights flickered dimly inside shops where goods lay strewn in the aisles, and blaster burns scored the counters. He passed by them all, only glancing inside and hurrying on. He thought he heard the faint crackle of bones behind him and the slither of movement across the dusty floors. He turned sharply, but there was nothing there, nothing but shadows. Still, he kept a cautious watch on his backtrail as he ascended the ramp. The tiny noises continued, but he couldn't catch the stalker.

The lights grew dim again as he passed through a residential quarter. Doorways hung open, showing sacked apartments and more of the brittle skeletons. Side corridors branched off from the main ramp, but Chael stayed on his chosen course. He was sure this ramp led to the top of the city, to the dome above the plaza. If there were a way out, it had to be up there. But he'd climbed for a long time, and the muscles of his calves and back protested the continual uphill hike. His belly rumbled, and he tried not to think of how long it had been since he'd eaten.

Then the scuttling sounded behind him, much closer than before. He whirled and saw a brown-furred back dash into the shadows. The stalker's eyes gleamed pale gold, level with his waist. Whatever hunted him, it was larger than he cared to face alone and unarmed. But he resisted the temptation to run. He was sure the beast would spring on him as soon as he turned his back. He knew he couldn't continue long in this backwards shuffle. He pushed at the closed doors as he passed, hoping for safety in one of the undamaged apartments. The first two doors refused to budge.

The brown beast, growing bolder, stood in plain sight in the center of the ramp. A row of bristles along its back were raised so that it had a stiff brush of hair running from the tip of its long, predatory snout to its short, round tail. The third door opened, and Chael stumbled through into a brightly lighted room and slapped his hand to the lock. The door vibrated under the impact of the hunter's heavy body. It threw itself again at the barrier, but the door held firm. He heard it snuffling outside, then silence. He was sure it had settled down to wait for him. Safe for the moment, he turned to examine the apartment.

"Lissa, you can't be serious about this!" Mave protested. She'd set aside her grief, knowing that she'd pay later for the rigid self-control, but she had to be ready to take advantage of any opportunity to reach this world's one com-link. But Lissa grew increasingly strange and seemed to have her own ideas about how to proceed.

"I think it suits me," she said, fastening her blonde hair into a knot with a bone pin. She wore a short cape of black fur and a mask of carved wood painted

with white lead that covered her forehead, nose and cheeks—a skull mask. She turned to Mave and laughed suddenly.

"If you could only see your expression! You look so grim."

"This isn't a joke," Mave said, trying to make Lissa understand. "These people take their magic seriously." And maybe it's more than magic, she thought, remembering the shaman's silver helmet.

"They take Kemmet seriously, too," Lissa replied coolly, "and she's agreed to make me their new priestess." She cocked her head. "Listen. The ceremony's starting." Lissa drew her cape around her and was gone, leaving Mave staring helplessly after her.

The first things to attract Chael's notice were the containers resting on a low table against the wall. He grabbed the largest and was rewarded by the sound of liquid sloshing inside. It looked temptingly like the water containers he'd used on Ozine Station, and those small, egg-shaped packages, surely they were food bulbs! Eagerly, he sorted through them. Some were black, but he found nine bulbs that were still pink and wholesome looking. He considered his find carefully. They might poison him or they might not, but he was certain to die soon if he didn't have food and water. He opened the water canister, and the wet, sweet smell reassured him. He drank eagerly. Then, more cautiously, he opened one of the bulbs and smelled the tart, pink meat. It seemed good, and he ate ravenously. No pains followed immediately upon the meal, and he felt better. In fact, he felt far more confident and energetic than he had since leaving the Wolf people's camp. He had to get out, get to the surface. He had food and water. Now, he needed a weapon. The watcher at the door would not give up easily.

The room beyond was small and bare. There were shelves with dishes on one side and a table with four chairs neatly placed around it. Chael tried the next door. This room was more crowded—two of the inhabitants hadn't escaped. Shut inside the sealed room, the bodies were better preserved than those on the ramp. The first man sprawled in an arm chair, right leg thrust out, left arm dangling, head thrown back. Half his chest was burned away. The skin had dried to a tough parchment that held all the bones in place. The dead man's dusty orange robe seemed almost new. The other figure lay stretched prone on the floor, head towards his victim. A broken knife blade protruded from his back, and his fingers curled around the barrel of a blaster.

Chael cried out and dove for the weapon. Here at last was a way to escape. If only the charge were still good! The brittle fingers snapped as he pulled the blaster away. The make was alien. The grip was a little too small for his hand but still usable. The barrel trembled as he aimed at the wall to the dining area. Brilliant white fire shot out and left a blackened hole in the wall. The charge was still nearly on full. He felt weak with relief. He wasn't safe yet, but he was no longer helpless, and he was a giant step closer to his goal. But first, he had to get by the beast that waited on the ramp.

Back in the main room, he stared thoughtfully at the door. He could just start blasting, but the hunter was fast and wily. He might miss, and he couldn't afford to waste the charge. There might be other weapons in this graveyard city, but he didn't have time to hunt for them. He pressed against the door, gradually ignoring the sound of his heartbeat, the sound of his breathing, the whisper of the breeze from the ventilator shafts.

He thought he heard a rustle and a low grunt from the other side of the door. The beast was very close. Quickly, he made up his mind. He untied the tunic sleeves from around his waist and slipped it on over his head. Returning to the other room, he grabbed the thin coverlet off the bed, then bundled the food bulbs and water container in it. He tied the ends of the bundle to form a bag that looped under his left arm and over his right shoulder. Burden securely in place, he held the blaster firmly in his right hand and hit the lock with his left. The door slid back.

The corridor seemed empty. Chael hesitated. He was sure he'd heard the beast, but now he couldn't see it. He took another step forward, then paused to listen again. The pause saved his life. The hunter, after waiting so long, lost patience with the prey. With a grunt, it let go its claw hold on the wall above the door and dropped in front of him.

Chael recoiled. The rank reek of fur and fetid breath choked him. The yellow eyes were centimeters from his own in the split second before he fired. The beast coughed, its eyes already glazing. The furry muzzle brushed his hand as it fell. Chael sighed as he squeezed past the body. The way ahead was clear, and he set off with determination, ignoring his aches and pains.

Eventually, the residential area gave way to more shops, but these vendors, with their dainty, discreet windows displayed goods far more luxurious than those below. In some windows, gems glittered and flashed, while others showed gleaming, exotic fabrics and artwork. This was truly the luxury sector, yet the looter hadn't reached here. None of the shops had been disturbed. Chael tried several doors and found them all securely locked. It would take special tools to break into one of these. Death must have come very quickly to the city.

One window displayed a tiny forest made of gems. Miniature trees twinkled with faceted flowers by a silver brook. The long dead artist had captured the essence of life in the tiny world. How many generations, he wondered, since any eyes had marveled at the jeweled forest? He might be the first to pass this treasure trove since the fall of the city. Any one of the items here would be worth a fortune to the finder—if he could keep them long enough to sell them. There was enough wealth here to buy a thousand ships. Chael's fingers crept to his father's medallion. If he lived—but there were many obstacles to be overcome first. It would take more time than he had to break into the shop. Resolutely, he turned his back on the dream and continued upward. But he'd be back.

The way was clear, and he made good time. The shop windows soon thinned, and he trudged through a district of smart, military barracks. Abruptly, he was on the verge of an ancient battlefield. Black scars marred the walls here, and skeletons lay in circles, as if making some desperate last stand. Cautiously, he skirted the teetering piles of rubble that edged the ramp, but soon he faced another dilemma. The giant laser that had cut the canyon on the plaza floor had scored here, too. The ramp was seared away so that only a narrow ledge, barely a hand's breadth wide, remained. There was no other way out.

He was tired, with little food or water left. Even if he went back down to the plaza to try another route, there was no guarantee that the new path would be any better. His mind made up, he began sliding along the ledge. His face was to the wall, the cold stonework numbing his cheek. Soon the air smelled wet, and he heard the trickle of water. There was a rumble, as of thunder, and he felt the vibration through the wall.

He moved steadily, mechanically, his breathing in

rhythm with his crab-wise steps. A fresh breeze blew past him, and he almost lost his grip. It was laden with the wet scent of growing things and earth—and a breeze from outside! He forced himself to keep to a steady pace. One slip now would end all their chances. At last, the ledge widened. Relieved, he turned, stretching his cramped muscles. His right hand shook, and his legs trembled. It was his metal hand that held him to the ledge. Ahead of him, a collapsed portion of roof lay under a muddy blanket. Small rivulets cut through the soil and dripped off the edge of the platform. He saw daylight at the top of the slope.

Chael scrambled up the hill. A burst of speed carried him up the slippery, muddy slope and out into the rainy, grey dawn. He stood in a shallow rock shelter watching a curtain of run-off drip from the bluff above. The sky glowed with pearl-grey light, and thunder rumbled quietly at the edge of hearing. The Kor-grass grew green and bright as far as he could see.

His knees buckled under him. He was exhausted, utterly weary. Fumbling, he untied the pack. The small pile of provisions he pushed back against the wall of the shelter. He drew the fabric over him and lay down. It was just after dawn, but dawn of what day he neither knew nor cared.

Jody leaned listlessly against the side of the cage. He'd long since ceased to feel the pain in his legs. Ona's head lolled against his chest, and she mumbled deliriously. He reached for the water skin and let a few drops trickle into her mouth. He'd refilled the bag during the torrential rain of the day before, or they'd now be even worse off. He almost wished for another downpour, despite the chill it brought. After hanging in the cage for so long, they were both filthy with dust, sweat, and their own excrement. With his survival conditioning, it would be a long time yet before he died, but Ona had fallen into a fitful fever. He thought the confinement hurt her more than the exposure. Gently, he brushed the long hair away from her face and tried to settle into a more comfortable position in the swaying cage.

It was dusk when Chael awoke. He ate the last of the food bulbs and drank the rest of the water, then took his bearings. Most of his journey had led upward, and he now stood near the cave where the cavi had tried to root him out. The narrow stream canyon was like a crack in the earth, and there, not far to the south, rested the bluffs above the Hawk people's camp. He didn't know how he was going to free Jody and Ona—one blaster wouldn't go far against the whole tribe—but he'd think of something. He had to.

At the back of his mind, a small hope flickered. Lissa was free. She'd eluded the Hawk warriors. Surely, she'd head straight for Mave and the Wolf people. But it was a long, difficult trip for one traveling alone. The help she brought might arrive too late, or she might never make it. There were worse things than the cavii lurking in this world, like the beast in the underground, he thought shuddering. He marched towards the camp, fighting the thick Kor-grass that barred his way.

Later, he was grateful for the grass. It hid him as he crawled toward the camp on his belly. The sky was dark and cloudy, but the flickering campfires were a sure guide. He altered his course slightly, hoping to go around the camp without rousing any guards and reach the cage unnoticed. He couldn't see Jody and Ona in the thick night, but he hoped that meant no one in the camp could see him either.

The darkness was full of unfamiliar noises, and odd, pungent smells reached him through the perfume of the Kor-grass. Then just ahead of him hung the angular silhouette of the cage. Cautiously, he crawled closer. He moved forward eight or ten meters with no trouble when, without warning, his head met a massive, fleshy obstruction, and he smelled the overpowering odor of cavii.

The frightened animal squealed and reared to its feet. Chael rolled back, but a glancing blow from a hind foot sent him tumbling helplessly through the grass. He cannoned into another cavi and bounced off. The second cavi squealed in turn, this time with the deeper pitch of an adult. Stunned, Chael lay in a limp huddle on the grass. All around him, he heard the thump and snort of cavii milling in the dark.

A youngster thundered by squealing shrilly, and the panic spread. Suddenly, the whole herd fled, and he felt the ground shake under their weight. The herd headed for the Hawk camp in one compact mass. Appalled, Chael stared after them. He was stunned but unhurt.

Above the thundering gallop, he heard the yells and screams of the nomads. The fires were scattered under the onslaught, and the flying embers fell on the tents, sending them flaring up one after another. The hide tents burned with black, greasy smoke stained red by the spreading fires. People ran like tiny manikins, fleeing the fire and the cavii.

Frightened anew by the fire, the herd milled in confusion. Single animals broke from the group and ran in random directions. A bull, bellowing with pain from the burn on its haunch, passed perilously near the cage. There was enough light from the burning tents for Chael to see Jody and Ona standing pressed against the bars. Forcing himself to move, Chael headed for them. A fractured rib grated at his side. He all but fell over the rope that held up the cage.

"Chael! Get us out of here!" Jody called.

"What's going on?"

"Accident," he said. It hurt to talk. "Explain later." The rope was wrapped several times around the support post and then tied in a complicated looking knot. It had taken six strong Ozine warriors to pull the cage up. Well, he was going to lower, not raise it, but the thing was going to come down with an almighty crash.

"Brace yourselves," he called, drawing the blaster. He wasn't going to waste time trying to untie the knot. He pulled the trigger. The white light flared briefly, but not nearly as bright as it should be. Had all the rain and knocking around ruined the mechanism? Chael kept his finger on the firing stud. The handle grew unbearably hot, but the rope started to smoke. He transfered the blaster to his metal hand. The barrel glowed white hot before the rope broke. The cage fell with a crash, landing on its side. Splintered wood shone white in the firelight.

"Open the door!" Ona commanded.

Chael hurried to obey. They scrambled out, half falling. Both prisoners were stiff after their long confinement, but they had to hurry.

"Come on!" Chael urged. "We've got to get away from here." The cavii were dispersing, and the Hawk people might catch sight of them at any moment.

"Grab the water bag," Jody called. Chael grabbed the half-full skin, and Jody snatched the crumbling loaves that remained in the basket. Chael took one last look at the orange-lit encampment. He thought he saw Tsada in her feathered cloak standing in front of a blazing tent. Then the smoke hid the camp, and they were running into the night.

"Lissa, I won't let you," Mave insisted. *"I forbid it!"*

"Who are you to forbid me anything?" Lissa demanded haughtily. *"Your time of power is past. You are nothing. You live by my sufferance."* She looked over a collection of ceremonial stone knives, choosing the one best suited to her purpose. The skull mask gleamed pallid white against her face.

"You can't sacrifice one of these people," Mave insisted. She knew the danger she courted, but she couldn't keep silent.

Lissa turned toward her. *"Do not try me too far."*

But Mave was past heeding any warnings. She knew that Lissa meant to go through with the sacrifice of one of the Wolf people to her own dark power, and no words would dissuade her. The chief trader moved quickly, striking low, but she was still weak, and it slowed her. The butt of the stone knife thudded against her skull, filling the world with white flashes of pain. Lissa watched her as she fell.

They stumbled on for hours. The Kor-grass made every step a trial. Chael's mouth was dry, but his clothes were drenched with sweat. He was tempted to open the bag and drink his fill, but there was no telling when they'd find more. He held the water skin under his arm and willed himself not to think. He was a border guard, son of a Rim Runner; he could go on forever. The tramp of his feet was so automatic that he didn't notice when the Kor-grass gave way to spongy tundra. He slogged on relentlessly, beyond pain or thought. The others stumbled beside him. There were all too tired to speak.

Gradually, the sky lightened. Ona reeled into him, and he stumbled and fell. The loose scree cut his hand. He felt a stupified wonder at the change in the ground.

Jody turned, swaying. Carefully, Chael climbed to his feet and helped Ona up. Her face was covered with sweat, her features pinched and drawn.

"We've got to find a place to rest," Jody said.

With an effort, Chael raised his eyes and surveyed the area. They were among the debris of some past glacier; huge grey boulders lay scattered along the gravel. A nearby pile offered the only shelter in reach. Chael dragged Ona's arm around his neck and lurched towards it.

It wasn't much. Two of the granite chunks had fallen close enough together to make a sort of wind break. Cold, hungry, and exhausted, they huddled in the shelter. Chael passed the water skin. Ona drank, then Jody. When Chael finished, less than a liter remained. They each chewed one of the cakes.

Chael ate his slowly, trying to make it last, but it was gone all too soon, leaving him feeling hungrier than ever. Then he could fight off the fatigue no longer. It washed over him in waves, like a drug. He curled up against Ona, spoon-fashion, with Jody huddled near. The gravel pricked his arm. He had a moment to feel the chill wind, and then he was asleep.

9

Consciousness returned to Chael with a tingling in his arm and the smell of frying meat. A sharp pang of hunger pricked him fully awake. He lifted his head from his arm and was rewarded with the pins and needles of returning circulation.

"What?"

"The returning hero awakes," Jody said. His red hair was filthy and matted, and his clothes were rags, but he still managed to smile. "How are you feeling this morning?"

Movement brought a host of new aches and pains from overtaxed muscles. Chael grimaced at the young trader.

"Terrible," he replied. Nevertheless, he sat up to see what Jody was cooking over the small, almost smokeless fire. Elongated blue shapes were spitted on a green stick. Chael sniffed.

"Fish—of a sort," Jody said informatively. "Ona's gone to get some more."

Just then the Wolf-witch returned. She carried three more of the wriggling blue "fish," although they had a lizard's legs as well as gills. Still, if Ona said they were edible . . . . His stomach felt as if it were wrapped around his backbone. At this point, he'd give anything a try. When Jody finally allowed him his share, he found the blue-white fish flaky and surprisingly sweet. The "fish" tasted more like baked fruit than meat, but it was hot and filling. Chael ate all his portion gratefully.

"What now?" he asked, licking his fingers after he'd finished. Ona had refilled the water bag from the pool where she'd found the fish. The water was brackish, but it took away their first.

"We go that way," Ona said, pointing west with her small chin. She looked still pale but she was remarkably recovered from yesterday's near-collapse.

"The camp is there," she said. "We must return to my people and bring them news of what has happened."

"Yes," Chael said ironically. "They won't have

94

to worry about war with the Hawk people now." Those few of Tsada's tribe who survived would be too busy staying alive to be any threat, if they ever had been. Ona seemed almost to read his mind.

"It is finished," she said. "But we are still alive and must go on."

"Mave is at the Wolf camp," Jody said, "and maybe Lissa made it back, too."

"Maybe," Chael said. All he could do was go on and hope that she still lived.

"All right," said Chael, standing up. It hurt to move. "Let's make for the camp."

They made the five-day march in three days. They marched like machines, and the ache of cold, over tired muscles became the normal background feel of his body. Ona knew where to find small game and occasional water. She made a sling from strips cut off her wolfskin cape and a couple of round stones. She even made the knife she used to cut the skins, chipping a piece of chert to a rough but serviceable edge.

They came to the Wolf camp at last on a drizzling morning with the wind spitting sleet in their faces. Chael's cheeks felt numb. The earth-walled houses seemed pitifully small and insignificant compared to the great city he'd seen—but this hamlet was alive. The slender forms of Ozine warriors gathered at the entrance to the main lodge. There was a shout as someone caught sight of them. A contingent of warriors came towards them at a lope, javelins at ready. Chael saw others scattering to protect the village. They stood still, Ona in the forefront, her tattered wolfskin robe thrown back over her shoulders. Jody looked ready to defend her if the warriors failed to treat her with due deference. Chael found himself automatically falling into the fighting stance long ago drilled into him. But tattered as she was, the warriors still recognized the wearer of the wolfskin cloak.

"Ona!" their leader exclaimed. She was a sinewy woman with old, white scars on her arms. "We were told you were dead."

"I am very much alive, as you can see," Ona replied. "As are the outlanders."

The leader gazed thoughtfully at them for a moment. Then she stepped forward and cupped Ona's chin in her palm, gazing into the girl's eyes.

"Yes, it is true," she said at last, releasing her. She made the same hypnotic inspection of both Jody and Chael. As her calloused palm cupped his chin, Chael had again that odd sense of identification, of belonging that he'd felt during the initiation rite.

"Sergeant, we are tired and hungry," Ona said. "Let us find shelter."

"At once," the Sergeant agreed. Her warriors formed a loose group around them as they entered camp. The rough sod houses seemed unreal to Chael. His mind still superimposed the delicate architecture, the lighted shop windows of the underground city. He remembered the jeweled garden—his key to freedom. Did it really exist on this ice-smothered world?

They were led into the council house. The hall was full, and Chael choked on the sudden reek of close-packed bodies. He'd been too long in the open air. Smoke stung his eyes, and he felt the unmistakable pull of stim. At the far end of the room, Balvar sat with Kemmet who looked far from pleased at the unexpected return of her sister.

"Who are these?" she asked haughtily. She clearly intended to make their return difficult.

"The witch Ona and two outlanders," the Sergeant replied stolidly.

"Indeed?" Kemmet drawled. She leaned back in her seat. Firelight flashed on her copper ornaments and on her white dress, made of the softest, finest suede. She looked at the three ragged travelers with distaste.

"I've tested them," the Sergeant maintained. "They are truly themselves, neither spirits nor strangers."

"That's impossible!" broke in a new voice. Lissa stood next to Kemmet, naked but for a black cape of wolf fur and a skull-like mask. Her body was creamy, voluptuous against the dark fur.

"Lissa!" cried Chael. He was suddenly, joyfully glad to see her alive; until he realized the meaning of her costume. She ignored him, staring at the Ozine behind them until the hall was still. Then she spoke with arrogant authority.

"Ona and the War Leader and the trader are dead," she stated emphatically. "I saw them die with my own eyes." She smiled then, that same cool, delicious smile of white teeth and blue-grey eyes.

Chael was stunned, yet somehow it was like Lissa to take advantage of the opportunity to play priestess. She waited for silence before she spoke again.

"Out with the imposters," she said imperiously. "Take them away."

"But I tested them," the Sergeant insisted. The warriors around them halted.

"You lie!" Lissa snapped, but she'd gone too far. She was a trader after all, and she hadn't been initiated.

"This woman doesn't belong to us," said the Sergeant, stung. "Why should we listen to her?" There were murmurs of agreement, and the Sergeant's warriors gathered around her, hands on their weapons. Kemmet intervened.

"Enough!" she ordered, as imperiously as any queen. She glared at the Sergeant. "You obey the stranger because she obeys me. Have I not made her Priestess?"

"Priestess!" Ona snorted. "That fat lump of grease has no more power than a suckling. How is she going to protect you? How is she going to speak to the spirits?" Ona turned to the crowd. "How is this outlander going to open the gates of power?"

"Enough!" Kemmet cried again. "Silence!"

But Ona wasn't through. Her yellow eyes blazed as she turned on her sister. "And what makes you think you have the power to make a priestess? Is your mind addled? I made myself priestess," she said emphatically, jabbing her thumb against her chest. "I, and I alone, assumed the power. You can't give anything to this stranger."

"I give what I please," Kemmet said icily, "and I take away what I please."

Balvar tried ineffectually to stop her. "Kemmet, you go too far," he said, but he was too late.

"Silence!" she hissed at him. "I'm tired of your mewling."

"Since your power is so great, dear sister," Ona sneered, "let us see how you use it. Let there be a test between your outlander witch and myself."

"Very well," Kemmet agreed, too angry to be cautious.

Chael saw Lissa go pale, but she made no move to protest. He wanted to warn her, but he couldn't speak. He didn't know what test Ona had in mind, but he was sure the Ozine witch would win the challenge. Lissa didn't know what she was up against. But he was silent, strung taut by the electric crackle of psychic power. Couldn't Lissa feel it? The trader moved forward confidently. She seemed like a beautiful, wild animal in the barbaric council house. Then Chael heard an exclamation behind him.

"Mave!" Jody cried. The boy stared at the tall, gaunt woman at the edge of the crowd. She was clad in ragged skins, and her face was bruised and dirty. Mave clearly hadn't prospered since Lissa's rise to power. The chief trader smiled once at Jody. The smile lingered a moment on Chael, but he was too torn by Lissa's plight to respond.

Lissa and Ona faced each other in the center of the open space between the chief's bench and the floor where most of the Wolf tribe sat. Lissa looked like a snow goddess as she faced Ona, and the Wolf-witch's ragged cape and wild black hair made her seem like some elemental night creature. Then the spectators parted to make way for the shaman. His red paint and furs seemed hastily donned, but the silver ball helmet was firmly in place. Briefly, Chael wondered which of the villagers this was. He didn't know the people well enough to tell who was missing. The shaman went straight to the space between the contestants and seated himself cross-legged on the floor. Chael saw Lissa raise one perfect eyebrow. She obviously didn't know the shaman's secret.

"Lissa," Chael cried, "it's a mirror." But he was pulled away before he could say more. Lissa deliberately turned her back on him. Helplessly, he watched as the contest began. The shaman's silver headdress seemed to cloud, and the room grew misty. He watched incredulously as Lissa's form flowed and changed. She grew taller, to half again her own height. Her bones were long, her skin taut. Silver claws tipped her fingers. She wore a necklace of human skulls, and each skull winked with diamond eyes. Smoky wraiths whirled around her. Her lips were red with fresh blood, and her face twisted into a smile that made him shudder.

But Ona changed too. She dropped to all fours as black fur covered her. The huge black wolf bared white fangs below yellow eyes—Ona's golden eyes, ferocious, intelligent, unchanged.

The two circled, looking for an opening, any weak place. The wolf leapt, and Lissa lunged with her clawed hands. Chael heard a snarl, a scream, saw the savage whirl of skin and fur. Then the two were apart. Lissa nursed one bleeding arm, but there were red streaks on the she-wolf's flank.

Warily now, they feinted. Lissa grew confident again. She let her guard drop almost contemptuously, as if inviting the other within range of her claws. Ona limped heavily, and the blood from her haunch fell in droplets on the floor. Lissa moved in, and Ona suddenly dropped her pretense of defeat. Her fangs fastened on the trader's throat. Her forelegs tangled in the necklace of skulls, splashed red now with Lissa's own blood. Lissa screamed hoarsely, clawing for the wolf's eyes, but Ona held on relentlessly.

Chael yelled, rushing to separate them. It was like running through thick mud, and it seemed to take ages to get close to them. Then suddenly, he fell on the writhing bodies. He grabbed the she-wolf by the throat, choking her in turn.

"Ona, stop it! Let go!" he yelled.

Lissa was on her knees, blue eyes closed. Her face was the color of snow. She seemed to shrink. The necklace disappeared, and Chael knew she was dying. He let go of Ona's throat. Raising his metal hand high over his head, he brought it down as hard as he could on the back of the she-wolf's neck. Her jaws let go as he hit home, and Lissa fell unconscious to the floor. The wolf become a woman again. Ona looked as if she too would fall. She was pale and swaying, but she remained standing. Chael could hardly believe that one so small and fragile seeming possessed such terrible strength. The shaman bent over Lissa.

"No!" Chael said. Whatever she'd done, she didn't

deserve any more of this alien trial. He was filled with disgust for the Ozine and all their ways. The shaman turned to him, and again Chael felt that sense of belonging. His fear and anger melted. Lissa was in no further danger. None of them were. His hands dropped to his sides, and his shoulders sagged. Ona too seemed worn out at last. She turned to Kemmet.

"We will retire now," she said. "Have a meal prepared for us." She turned and limped out, Chael stumbling in her wake. Jody followed, but not before he and Mave had organized bearers to carry Lissa with them. They retired to a house on the outskirts of the village, and retainers hurried to make them beds of soft furs, while others brought platters of meat and glasses of hot, sweet ale. Chael ate and drank without tasting. His body needed fuel, and he would feed it so that it wouldn't disturb him in his rest. The furs might have been coarse grass for all he felt them. He was asleep instantly.

10

"Hold her head up a little higher," Mave said, as she spooned the soup into Lissa's mouth. Lissa swallowed automatically, with no sign that she knew what she was doing. Chael shifted his position, careful not to let her head fall back too far. Her skin was clammy, and he felt reluctant to touch her—she whom he'd once wanted so much. But now, the vision of the clawed monster intruded everytime he looked at her. He watched as Mave wiped Lissa's chin and fed her another spoonful of soup.

"Why are you so kind to her?" he asked. "Why not let her die?" Death seemed preferable to this blasted parody of life.

Mave looked surprised. She was still far too thin, but now she at least had clean, warm clothes. Her period of captivity was ended.

"It's my duty," she answered simply. "She is sworn to my Household."

"Even now?"

"Even now," she agreed. "She's injured, helpless. I must see her placed in a proper med-center before I can end the obligation."

Privately, Chael doubted whether a med-center would be able to do much for Lissa. She seemed to have no direction, and her vacant expression showed no evidence of will or intelligence. He'd seen that blank look before, on Haldar's younger brother after they dug him out of the collapsed bunker. He'd had food and water and good air, but three weeks in darkness and silence had broken his mind. He'd been like a huge doll afterwards, moving where he was led, staying where he was put, even as Lissa now rose obediently when he urged her. Mave brought a robe and leggings, and dressed her. Lissa seemed not to notice. Chael felt no desire for her now. The smooth curves of her body aroused him no more than the curves of a carved figure.

"Will you watch her please, Chael?" Mave asked as she fastened Lissa's cloak. She frowned anxiously. "I know this is hard for you, but I must talk to Kemmet. There is a chance she may let us go now."

"Hard for me! What about for you?"

"I can't abandon her so long as she's injured, no

matter what she's done. In any case, I'd never leave one of my Household stranded among aliens,'' Mave said. ''I'll be back soon.''

So Chael was left alone with Lissa who sat and stared mindlessly through him. The air seemed like lead. He couldn't breathe. Lissa with her mind broken—she sat so still—worse than dead. He sobbed angrily, surprising himself, and choked on hot, bitter tears. He hid his head in his hands, unable to hold in his grief any longer. He didn't hear Mave return.

''Chael! Oh, poor Chael,'' she said. ''I should have known better.'' She sat next to him, and her warm arms went around his shoulders. He turned to her and wept while she murmured comfort, rocking him back and forth like a child. After a time, he stopped, ashamed of his loss of self-control. Haldar would have scorned him for a fool. No woman was worth mourning, especially not one as treacherous as Lissa. His head was still cradled between Mave's neck and shoulder. He felt the soft pressure of her breasts and her hand on his hair. He pulled away from her and sat up straighter, unable to meet her eye.

''I've been an idiot,'' he said.

''No,'' Mave said. ''Just human.''

He looked at her quickly, but she wasn't mocking him. But before he could speak more, they were startled by a loud argument outside. Ona's voice rose above the babble.

''I won't have them here,'' she insisted.

Chael and Mave emerged to see a crowd gathered in the open space in the middle of the village. They pushed through the mob to the center of the storm. The Hawk people had arrived—what was left of them. This remnant represented only about a quarter of the people Chael had counted in their camp. He felt sick. He heard a hoarse voice call his name. The voice belonged to an old woman clad in ragged fur with raw, red burn scars on her arms and face. Only the dark eyes were as he remembered them.

"Tsada!" He dropped to his knees beside her. "Tsada, I'm sorry. I didn't mean . . . ."

"It is done," she said, silencing him. "Do not grieve. We eat now, and we have a fire to keep us warm. The chief's wife favors us."

"I do not favor you, old woman," Ona interrupted. "I say you go. At once!"

"No!" Chael protested. He stood up to face the Wolf-witch.

"Silence, you fool," Ona ordered. "Your tender reunion with this old she-cavi is very touching, especially when I remember how carefully she made us a sacrifice to that carrion eater she calls upon."

"Your tongue is loose, girl," Tsada said. "You speak as a child who knows only the force of her own will. But I am mistress of powers unknown to you. Do not try me too far."

"Talk," Ona sneered. "All talk, and to no purpose. You and your band of thieves will go now."

"They stay," Chael said fiercely. He'd had enough of Ona's boastful cruelty.

"I am mistress here," Ona began.

"I would disagree with you on that point, sister." Kemmet emerged from the circle of warriors. Her white dress was in spotless contrast to the refugees' rags. "You are not chief here yet," she said.

"By the gods, you are not!" Balvar concurred, standing behind his wife. "And neither are you, woman," he added to Kemmet. "I rule here." And the heretofore silent warriors around them agreed.

"Balvar! Balvar!" they shouted, pounding their spearbutts on the ground. Chael was surprised at the display of loyalty, but perhaps they were as tired as he was of the sisters' arrogance.

Kemmet and Ona glared at the chief in shared hostility. It was Tsada who broke the impasse. Slowly and painfully, she rose to her feet. She took the length of wood she carried for a staff and smacked it once against the ground in homage to Balvar.

"Chief of the Wolf people," she said, her voice no longer hoarse, but powerful and smooth. "I am Tsada, the Hawk-witch. I have brought my people to you to seek your protection and rulership. I place them in your hands as a trust." She paused. "And I offer my services as a witch."

"We don't need you," Ona said. Jody tried to silence her, but she shrugged him off.

Tsada didn't look at her, didn't let her eyes leave Balvar's. "What use is a girl?" she asked reasonably. "Can a girl give you sage council? Can a girl support you in the assembly? Can a mere girl command the powers that I command?" Balvar made no defense of Ona.

"Don't look at her, you fool," Ona hissed. "She's stealing your mind."

Kemmet turned on her in rage. "Have you no respect? We are not led by a fool." She seemed to forget her own past comments. Ona had gone too far at last. Jody looked frightened for her.

Tsada turned to Ona and spoke with great authority. "You did battle last week, and you were wounded—by a novice. Your tricks have served you well enough among those who have no talent, but I can crush you. You are a child. But because of your youth and for the sake of my friend, Chael, I will let you live. But not here. You must go away. Go with these outlanders, and trouble me no more."

"No!" Ona cried.

Balvar turned on her. "What she says is true. You

are a child, and this Hawk-witch is more powerful. Go.''

Ona went white. She was suddenly pitiful as she turned to her sister. ''Kemmet, Please!''

''Balvar is right,'' Kemmet said. She looked afraid herself. Two could go into exile as easily as one.

''I won't go!'' Ona cried. But Tsada turned to her and raised her hands high over her head. Ona covered her eyes and screamed. Jody caught her as she fell.

''What have you done?'' Mave demanded.

''She is not hurt,'' Tsada said as she lowered her hands. ''Who knows? The lesson may even do her good. Take the child with you, outlander. Chael tells me you wish to return to the place where the Ozine live. Perhaps they will take her in.'' She glared at Jody. ''Or perhaps your brother will keep her. She cannot stay here. Journey well.''

Tsada turned away. The interview was over. Chael felt confused; nothing ever happened as he expected it to. Mave stood near him, looking very tired. He took her hand, and they followed Jody as he carried Ona back to their hut.

They left the next morning, and Ona was with them. They started off at sunrise, before the perpetual cloud cover was fully light. At first, Chael was afraid they'd have two mind-blasted casualties to shepherd across the tundra. Ona seemed dazed, but Jody looked after her, seeing that she ate at meal times, covering her at night. Gradually, she improved, but she was still subdued. Chael suspected that the sentence of exile affected her more than Tsada's blow to the mind. Ona had run smack into reality for the first time in her life. Mave continued to look after Lissa, but the renegade trader showed little improvement. Chael avoided them both, feeling guilty but unable to help himself.

This afternoon they lay belly down on the damp ground—except for Lissa who remained alone in the small camp they'd set up. She'd be as safe there as anywhere, Chael had argued, and Mave had given in reluctantly. They had to eat, and they couldn't bring Lissa along on the hunt. Ona had spotted a small herd of teppa nearby. They stalked them, stone-pointed spears in hand. Chael doubted he'd get close enough to use his weapon. He couldn't match Ona's or Mave's quiet competence. The teppa were at the head of a small box canyon, grazing on the tundra moss. The idea was to drive them into the canyon and trap them against the far wall. There, they could kill the confused animals at their leisure.

Chael clutched his spear and inched forward. He looked for Jody, but couldn't see him. Jody was supposed to circle around the teppa downwind and spook them into movement, but Chael wasn't sure how effective the maneuver would be. The tappa pawed delicately at the moss with their wide clawed feet. Occassionally, one snorted, and the others answered. Where was Jody? Was his scent so alien that the teppa just ignored him? But no, they were lifting their heads. Their long necks craned as they strove to identify the intruder. A calf moved closer to its dam. Chael heard Jody clap his hands and yell.

It was too much for the herd. They abandoned their moss and turned towards the plains, but they weren't to escape so easily. Ona leapt in front of them, shrieking and brandishing her spear. Two of the adults evaded her, but the calf was confused by the noise. Bellowing, it ran straight into the box canyon, and its terrified dam raced after it. The hunting party followed more slowly.

Chael arrived in time to see Ona take aim and thrust her spear expertly between the ribs of the calf. It bellowed again and fell to its knees. All four of the hunters yelled, and the teppa cow roared in outrage. The sounds bounced back and forth in the narrow canyon, making a blood-chilling racket. The cow charged Ona. The witch's spear was still stuck fast in the calf. They hadn't found enough wood to make more than one apiece. She dodged, but there was little room to move at the end of the canyon.

Mave thrust her spear at the cow's flank. It went in the length of the head, and then tore out of her hands. The cow charged again, and again Ona dodged. Jody stepped between them and thrust too. His spear glanced off the tough hide, leaving only a bloody furrow. The enraged cow turned on him. He jumped aside, but his foot slipped, and he fell heavily. The teppa moved to finish him.

"Jody!" Ona screamed.

Chael alone had a weapon left. He tried to remember his instruction in antique weapons, as he ran towards the young trader. Left foot forward, twist and thrust, don't forget the follow-through; he could almost hear his instructor's voice. The spear went in the teppa's lungs, sinking half-way up the shaft. The cow gave one last roar of anguish. Her knees buckled, and she fell slowly, majestically on to her side.

Jody looked up at him with a dazed grin of thanks. Ona knelt beside the boy, an anxious expression on her face. So, Chael thought, maybe it wasn't all one way after all.

"Thank you, Chael," Mave said.

He shrugged. There hadn't been any choice.

"Well, what do we do now?" Jody asked practically, as he got up.

"We butcher them," Ona replied.

The butchering proved to be a messy job. Chael had never hunted anything so large before, and the amount of blood and flies amazed him. The insects were like tiny, sage-green motes that flew in clouds so thick he was afraid he'd breathe them in. They slit the gut and hauled out the intestines to keep the meat from spoiling while they worked. Then, under Ona's direction, they skinned the teppa, first the cow and then the calf.

Chael swore as his hands slipped yet again on the bloody hind quarters, and he scraped his knuckles with the flint chopper. What he wouldn't give for a good laser knife, he thought. Next to him, Mave hauled on the bone as he chopped. She was covered with blood, sweat, and dirt. Her red hair was matted and filthy. She smiled at him, undaunted.

That night they ate chunks of teppa seared over the moss fire. The meat was tough, but the flavor was surprisingly good. At last, Chael licked his fingers clean and lay back, replete. His shoulder touched Mave's where they leaned against a convenient rock.

"Get enough to eat?" he asked.

"Mummmm . . . ." she answered.

"How's Lissa?"

"Asleep." Her voice was drowsy.

"You should be, too," he said. Tentatively, he put his arm around her. She moved closer, resting her head on his shoulder.

"What do you plan to do if we get off this planet?" she asked.

"I don't know," he said slowly. "Help rescue your Household, I guess."

"But then what?"

"Back to the stim vats, I suppose." The underground city was too private a dream to share just yet.

"You remember that I asked if you'd join my Household?"

"But I'm not a trader."

"You don't have to be born a trader," she replied.

She sighed and moved closer. Chael was silent. Mave was offering the best she had, far more than he'd find elsewhere, but did he want it? Mave's Household reminded him too much of the Guard; heirarchy, authority, obedience. He wanted to be free to fly from star to star following his own will, not another's order, not even Mave's.

"I'm honored . . . ," he began, but she put her finger on his lips.

"Don't answer now," she said. "Just think about it." She took her hand away and kissed him, then rose swiftly and went to her bed on the far side of the fire.

Think about it! But instead, he thought of starships and the underground city, and the gleaming, jeweled tree that would buy his freedom, if he could just reach it again. He closed his eyes.

They moved steadily north. The wind grew colder and the clouds thicker. There was snow on the ground and dirty grey ice in the hollows. Chael shivered and pulled his jacket closer. He couldn't remember being warm. His lungs ached from the icy air. Even Ona had donned warm, fur-lined clothing.

"Why couldn't they have put this benighted post further south?" he asked, panting.

"They probably wanted to stay out of tribal territory," Mave answered. "I suppose it's not so bad in full summer."

He scrambled up another icy slope where dark roots stuck out like frozen fingers. He couldn't imagine summer here.

"Ayyahh!" Mave cried. She slid backward on the ice, flying towards him. He threw up his arms to catch her, and she hit him with her full weight. They slid down the path at speed. Chael dragged his heels, trying to slow them. Pain flared in his back as he slid over roots and rocks. He slewed sideways and grabbed onto the projection. They jerked abruptly to a halt. For a moment, they lay still, shaken by the fall.

"Mave," Jody cried. "Are you all right?" He clambered down the path at a reckless pace. Ona watched from above, near the sledge. Lissa didn't stir.

"I'm all right," Mave said. "Slow down, Jody, you'll break your neck."

Jody stopped, waiting for them on the path. They disentangled themselves and started back up.

"Thank you, Chael," she said. She smiled. "I seem to be always saying that to you."

"It doesn't matter," he answered gruffly. He was thinking of how unexpectedly soft she felt against him. Was there a chance that he could ever be more than just another member of her Household? Then he noticed her limping.

"Are you sure you're not hurt?" he asked.

"Positive."

Their party continued across the ice, and soon they came to an area of loose gravel and scattered boulders. Chael didn't know which was worse, the gravel or the ice. He hated them both impartially. His fingers were numb. He coughed and blinked his watering eyes. It started to snow in long, slanting white streamers. Jody and Ona pulled the sledge. They were already half hidden. But where was Mave? He looked back and spotted her several meters behind them, a shadowy figure in the snow. He headed back towards her. She was leaning against a boulder as he came near. Her face was white, the skin drawn tight with pain.

"What's wrong?"

"Nothing," she said. "Go on. We must not get separated."

Chael snorted. "Am I supposed to leave you here to add your bones to the scenery?"

111

"Go on."

He ignored the order, grabbing her arm and pulling her forward. She took one step and almost fell as her weight came down on her right ankle. She cried out in pain.

"You were hurt. Why didn't you say so?" The wind howled around them. Jody and Ona were out of sight. He had to yell to be heard. "You could have ridden in the sledge."

"You couldn't pull both Lissa and me. We'd be too heavy together."

Chael glared at her, angry that she should think so little of herself. It was true they wouldn't have made much progress, but they could have tried. If they had to abandon anyone, he wouldn't choose Mave. Damn the woman and her crazy sense of honor. She was about to get them both killed. He couldn't see the others at all.

"Come on." He dragged her forward again, her arm over his shoulders. She lurched, and they fell together in the snow. Chael looked again for the sledge, hoping the others had noticed they were missing and come back to look for them. There was no sign of it. The snow fell in thick, wave-like drifts. He had to do something soon, or they'd both freeze. He took hold of Mave, and half crawling, half dragging her, managed to reach a group of boulders he remembered seeing at the edge of the path. He fell over them, rather than found them.

"In here," he said, dragging Mave into what shelter there was between the rocks.

"Hurry!"

"I can't," she said.

He heaved her forward and shoved on her rear. She cried out and fell down between the boulders. Chael struggled out of the heavy fur cape. It billowed like a sail, and he snatched it with both hands. His right hand lost its grip, but the metal one held. The cold didn't affect it. Cursing, he crawled into the meager shelter and pulled the cape on top of them. He pulled Mave close, wondering if they'd freeze to death before the storm ended.

11

He awoke from a dream of a warm bed. His hand was warm, but his joints ached. A ray of sunlight stabbed him in the eyes. He winced and turned away, his neck making a gritty noise, like sand in bearings. Mave lay in his arms, her chin tucked into his shoulder. His left arm was afire with pins and needles. He tried to wiggle his arm out from under her without waking her. She snorted once, startled, and opened her eyes. They were like twin green pools only centimeters from his own.

"What's going on?" she asked drowsily.

"We had a suicide pact, remember?"

"A what! Oh, the storm."

She moved her head, and he ground his teeth. She got up slowly. She must feel as stiff as he did. He used his right hand to pick up his left arm and rubbed briskly. At least the metal part didn't hurt.

"Here. Let me help," Mave said. Her fingers were strong and sure. It was agony. He gritted his teeth and closed his eyes. After a long while, the tingling subsided, and he could breathe again.

"How's your ankle?" he asked when she'd finished.

She peeled back her legging to look at it. The skin was discolored by a purplish bruise, but there was no swelling.

"Just a bruise," she said, regarding it critically.

"You can't go far on that."

"I'll manage." She refastened the legging, lacing it tightly to give as much support as possible. Chael stood up and tried to spot the sledge. He saw only virgin snowfields. They might have been the only people in the world. Their chance of survival was nil, but he wasn't going to let that stop him.

"Are you ready?" he asked.

She nodded, and they started off at a slow, steady pace. Mave limped, but not so badly as yesterday. They followed the shallow valley that led to the pass. The snow was only up to mid-calf here—the wind had blown most of it against the valley walls—but it was still hard going. They were almost on top of the sledge before they saw it. As they rounded a shallow bend, it lay directly in their path. It had been turned up endwise to make a shelter from the wind. Chael saw a slender figure with dirty blonde hair huddled at the leeward side.

"Chael! Mave!" Jody's shout of welcome echoed from the slopes. A small drift shook loose and rolled down beside them.

"Not so loud," Chael warned. "You'll bury us."

Jody looked startled, then ran to meet them. He embraced them both in a relieved bear-hug.

"Ona's looking for you," Jody said. "But she should be back this way soon. She's making a circle."

"Good," Chael grunted. "In the meantime, how about some food?"

Jody dug out some dried teppa. It was tough and rank, but they ate it anyway.

"Did anyone feed Lissa?" Mave asked.

"I boiled some of that stuff up in snow water for her this morning," Jody said. "She ate it all right."

Chael looked at Lissa. She huddled in the shelter of the sledge, chewing on the ends of her dirty hair. Her face was red and chapped. He felt pity for her, although he didn't want to feel anything.

"Let's get set up," Chael said. Lissa had only gotten what she deserved. "We'll want to get moving as soon as Ona comes back."

Quickly, they righted the sledge and packed their meager belongings. Jody started to lead Lissa to her usual seat.

"No," Chael said. "She can walk. Mave's hurt her ankle."

"There's no need . . . ." Mave protested.

"If you are hurt, you should ride," Ona interrupted. They turned to see her standing on the path behind them. "The other one can walk if led."

"She's right," Jody agreed, looking anxiously at Mave.

Reluctantly, Mave allowed herself to be overruled.

Chael took Lissa's hand and pulled her along after him. She went willingly enough for the first kilometer, but her pace soon slackened. They fell further and further behind. At last, she stopped completely. The sledge was far ahead, and Chael was in no mood to spend another night on their backtrail.

"This is no time to stop," he said.

Lissa ignored him, staring stonily ahead. Chael reached the end of his temper. Grabbing her arm, he started off at a fast march. Lissa went unwillingly, or so it seemed. He wondered how much her blasted brain understood. She fell once, but got to her feet again. Chael was in too much of a hurry to notice this first sign of independent action. They caught up with the sledge at the top of the next crest.

"Look!" cried Jody, pointing. Below them nestled half-a-dozen domes, covered with snow, but still unmistakably the product of human civilization.

Chael still had a not-quite-real feeling as he grasped a steaming mug of caff and waited for his shivering to subside so that he could drink it. Funny how he hadn't felt cold until he'd come into the comfortable warmth of the station. The Rim Runner who ran the post had been almost comically surprised to see them suddenly appear on his doorstep. But he recovered quickly, urging them inside. He was at the kitchen unit now, ripping the tabs off food packs and throwing them into the micro-oven. The smell of hot stew drifted to Chael, and his stomach growled. Later, as he ate, he noticed that Lissa had moved closer to the kitchen unit. He didn't remember anyone moving her. He watched her carefully, but she remained blank-faced as the Rim Runner spoonfed her.

The shuttle arrived in two days, and they made their way to Edris with no difficulty. Mave's credit was good on any civilized world. Chael enjoyed the novel sensation of traveling in comfort and warmth. They split up at the Edris spaceport.

"You and Ona must go to the Council," Mave said, "and tell the traders what has happened. Make them aware of the danger. We dare not let the Dan go unchecked."

Obediently, Jody and Ona caught the next ship headed for the Galactic west, and Tura, the traders' world where their one city nestled like an alien child on the barren wastes. Ona looked more exotic than ever in her blue jumpsuit. She appeared too fragile to bear the weight of even the small pack she carried, and she seemed subdued by her strange surroundings. But Jody was ready to help her. The young trader obviously relished his role as guide and tutor as a welcome change after so long in the opposite role.

Chael hoped they'd make it to Tura without trouble, or at least without encountering any problems Jody couldn't handle. His own role he wasn't so sure of. He and Mave were going to Shadriss, the nearest major world of the League, to gain support and ships. They were dressed accordingly, in conservatively cut but luxurious shipsuits. Discreet jewels twinkled at their necks and wrists. Lissa accompanied them, once more deep in her mindless trance. She wore a white hospital suit, indicating that she was an invalid. Mave planned to leave her at the med-center on Shadriss. She'd receive the best possible care there, and the chief trader would be free of her obligation. Chael wasn't sure if he wished for Lissa's recovery or not. Clean and dressed in civilized clothing, she looked as she had when he'd first met her. If she recovered, she faced sure disgrace. No trader would ever take a renegade into her Household. No man of her people would have her. Unless she got work on one of the League ships on one of the smaller lines, she'd be planetbound. The type of offer she was likely to get wouldn't appeal to one as proud as Lissa. Maybe it was better for her to remain mindless.

They boarded their own transport that afternoon. Mave had reserved a large suite for the three of them, and Chael wondered briefly how many credits this luxury had set her back. Once in their suite, he took off his tight new boots, wriggling his toes in the soft, white plush of the carpet. He dialed a bottle of his favorite red wine. The chair embraced him warmly as he sat down, and he sighed as it began massaging the kinks out of his back. He heard the whisper of cloth as Mave approached.

"That should take care of her for now," she said,

sitting opposite him. She looked regal in a shipsuit of royal blue Kanin velvet. A diadem of saphires circled her head, and a white lace jabot frothed at her neck. He poured another glass of wine and handed it to her.

"I know you think I'm a fool for not leaving her among the barbarians," she said defensively, taking the glass. "But I couldn't . . . ."

"You don't have to justify yourself to me," Chael said. "You did what you had to."

An uncomfortable silence followed, and Chael wondered if he should pour her another glass of wine. Maybe getting drunk would help her. He knew the chief trader well enough by now to know that she seldom—if ever—relaxed enough to forget her sense of duty. When he looked up, she was staring fixedly at the toes of her boots. Anyone seeing her would think that Mave, not Lissa, was the guilty one, he thought.

"I mean it," he said. She looked up, saying nothing. He wasn't getting through. "You have your ethics, and you're tough enough to stick to them. I respect that. But you've got to let go sometime."

She smiled slightly. "Is that how you think of me?" she asked. "Tough? Stern?"

"Well, no, not exactly." He felt more uncomfortable by the moment. "But your sense of duty may kill you yet."

She raised one eyebrow. "I'll keep that in mind."

"Anyway," Chael said, "they aren't barbarians, not completely."

"Oh?"

"Didn't you guess?" he asked. "It's Ozine Home!"

"Impossible."

"It's true. I swear it." The story of the underground city spilled out of him. He'd meant to keep it back,

118

but now he felt Mave was the one person he could trust with it.

"You're sure the city was native?" Mave asked at last.

"It was," he affirmed. "And there was the stim too. It was raw, not processed the way they do at Ozine Station, but still stim."

"This will bear thinking on," Mave said. "If the Wolf people are indeed Ozine, then Ona . . . ."

"The Regenetrix!" Chael exclaimed.

"Exactly."

They stared at one another, united by the secret they shared.

He woke, staring into the dark. Some rat-scratch of sound had stirred him. He lay still, listening. There was silence for a moment, then he heard it again—the scrape of soft boots across the plush carpet just behind him. It set off loud, clear danger signals in his brain. With a yell, he rolled over, throwing himself at the intruder. He grabbed a sinewy wrist, but the other twisted like a cat. The point of a knife slid like fire along his ribs. He yelled again and lunged, but a low table tripped him, and he crashed painfully among hard-edged furniture.

"Chael! What is it?" Mave called. He heard her run towards his door.

"Look out!" He cried. "He's got a knife."

There was a short scream and another crash. He untangled himself from the furniture and slapped his hand on the reostat. Light flooded the suite. Mave lay crumpled in the hallway.

"Mave!" He dropped to his knees beside her. She groaned and raised herself on one elbow.

"I'm just winded," she said, clutching her stomach.

119

But Chael drew her arm away to make sure. No blood, he was relieved to see. He helped her to her feet and to a low sofa. He quickly checked the suite. The front door stood wide open. There wouldn't be anyone in the hall by now, but he looked anyway. The passage was empty. He checked Lissa's room and breathed a sigh of relief when he saw her sleeping peacefully in her bed, the covers tucked under her chin like a small child. He checked the rest of the rooms to make sure, but the intruder was gone. He went back to Mave and found her still sitting on the sofa, pale but looking better.

"No one around?" she asked.

"Not a soul." He dropped into the chair next to her. "Shall I call security?"

She shook her head no. "And tell them what? It would only stir up unwanted interest. So far, the Dann don't even know we're alive. Let's keep it that way."

"They could already know," Chael said. "Our visitor might not have been just a simple thief."

"How could they?" she asked. She pulled her sheer robe around her, shivering. "No, it was a thief, and you surprised him before he could take anything. I don't think he'll be back."

Reluctantly, Chael gave in. He still thought Mave had passed the matter off too lightly, but he'd learned it was no use to argue with her once she'd made up her mind. Instead, he resolved to keep his eyes and ears open during the rest of their voyage. But nothing more happened, and the Tigris set down on the plains of Shadriss without incident. Chael had made good use of the travel tapes during his trip, so he was prepared for the dry, flat land and the strip of green bordering the river Ur. The rectangular towers and boxy houses painted in soft colors seemed almost familiar to him. What he wasn't prepared for, as he rode into the city in a small, open car, was the stench.

Fuel fumes and perfume blended with the odor of human and animal excrement, old vomit, sweat, and the delicately sweet scent of sage from the hedges. He tried breathing through his mouth, but the air coated his tongue with a thick, strange taste. He noticed that Mave too was looking ill. The only one unaffected by the assault was Lissa. She sat serenely, revealing nothing.

Their first stop was the med-center. It was a large white building with bright red doors and shutters. The colors reminded Chael of fresh blood and bandages, but the inside was cheerful enough. The windows let in floods of light, and there was a fountain in the middle of the lobby. Chael waited while Mave turned their ward over to the white-coated attendants. The official forms were quickly filled out and sealed with Mave's thumb print. Together, they walked back to where the car waited for them.

"You did the right thing," Chael said as they climbed in.

Mave turned to him. "Did I?" she asked.

He slammed the door and signaled the driver to move. "There's no need for this mourning," he said harshly. "She was a traitor."

"She could have been so much more . . . ."

"Well, she wasn't. She got better from you than she deserved. So drop the morbid guilt. All right?"

She sighed, then took his hand. "All right," she agreed.

Jody set the rented scout down expertly on Tura's one landing field. Ona waited silently while he went through the final formalities and shut down.

"This is your home?" she asked as they descended the ramp.

"In a way," he replied, glancing around at the horizon circumscribed by dericks and bales of cargo. "Tura is the home of my people, but I don't really have a home of my own."

She stopped abruptly. "Are you an exile, too?"

"No," he said, taking her arm. "I choose not to be bound to any one place. That's how most traders live."

"How very strange," she said.

They boarded a small ground transport and headed for the government offices. Jody frowned. The Council was in session, but whether they could be made to listen was another matter.

Chael, in his innocence, had thought that raising help on Shadriss would be a quick and simple matter. He was soon made aware of the intricacies of League politics. The officials had to be bribed in order of precedence, beginning with the junior minister for foreign trade. The voyage to the top was long and expensive. Chael bridled his temper as best he could, but he was under a continual seige of impatience. It was all very well for Mave to say this was the only way. He still chafed. To fill in the time, he took to exploring the port on foot.

Shadrissport was a sprawl of buildings alternating between splendor and squalor, with squalor dominating. Their hotel stood in well-tended grounds within three blocks of the Chancellor's palace, and for another twenty minute's walk away from the palace, the neighborhood remained park-like and prosperous. Then the real port began. The grassy lawns became parched plazas where refuse blew with a continual chatter. Shadowy figures lurked in crumbling doorways, waiting for nightfall like nocturnal animals. He strolled down Moon Street at dusk, ignoring the hucksters and hawkers, the pretty boys, and the women with bare breasts. Solitary, unaffected, he wandered like a dreamer.

He found a bar where Moon Street crossed Blackwater Alley. There was no name to mark it, only a sullen spill of light from the half-open door and the sound of loud voices within. He went inside and took a table at the back of the room. A woman came to take his order. Her greasy hair was piled in an elaborate coiffure, and her bare breasts lolled listlessly. She eyed his elegant black velvet tunic expertly, and smiled with the automatic come-on of a whore down on her luck.

"Racheff," Chael said briskly, ordering the local brandy. It burned like lye going down and produced a lethal hangover, but at least he could afford to pay for it himself. He'd pawned his silver battle medals for nearly 50 credits.

"That all you want?" the woman asked. She stood close to him, and he smelled sweat and cheap perfume.

"That's all," he said firmly.

She brought him the glass and set it down on the table with a slap that brought some of the dark brown liquid sloshing over. He sighed and paid her. She swished off as he examined the graffiti on the table top. Most of it was in the local alphabet and unreadable. He raised his eyes. Over in the opposite corner a group of men huddled over a carved board, their attention to the game blocking out everything else in the room, including the argument going on just at their backs.

"I paid!" the drunk insisted with loud sincerity. His jowels trembled. His paunch slipped further over his belt. The boy with him stepped back fastidiously.

"You paid only half, you drunken sot," the boy said clearly. He looked too young to be out on his own, and he seemed cleaner and better dressed than anyone in this neighborhood.

"I'll make it up to you. Just come with me," the other pleaded.

"No."

"Please, Avrill," the older man said, laying his hand on the boy's sleeve. The boy jerked away, hissing.

"Keep your hands off me!"

But the drunk surged forward, enfolding the boy in a flabby embrace. Avrill tried to twist away, but the other kissed him passionately. Chael found himself out of his seat and across the room before he knew what he was doing. The drunk slammed into the wall with a thud that rattled the glasses behind the bar. Chael stood poised, waiting for a countermove, but the other stared glassy-eyed and slid down to the floor. Chael turned to see Avrill watching him wide-eyed.

"Thank you," the boy said quietly.

Chael was suddenly aware of the silence all around him. He very carefully ignored the rest of the bar.

"You're welcome," he said. He turned and went back to his seat. The normal noises resumed. Avrill followed him, sitting down at his table. The boy smiled. His teeth were dazzling white.

"You must be a very strong man," Avrill said, edging closer. He put his hand on Chael's crotch and squeezed gently.

Chael removed the questing hand. "No thank you," he said firmly. Would he never learn to mind his own business?

"For you, I'd even go half-price," Avrill said. This time he ran his hand down the back of Chael's trousers. Chael jumped and blurted the first lie that came to him.

"I don't have any money," he said.

"None?" Avrill asked, withdrawing his hand. He pouted.

"I used my last credit to buy this drink," Chael lied.

Avrill sighed once, looked at him narrowly, and rose to go. "Come back when you have money, love," he said, not unkindly. Then he headed for the still prostrate drunk.

Chael felt his face flaming. He glanced around, but no one seemed interested in the exchange. He gulped down the rest of his brandy, hardly noticing as it burned its way down. Quickly, he headed for the door. Avrill didn't even see him go.

Once outside, he felt better. Well, it wasn't the first time he'd made a fool of himself. He ought to head back for the hotel. He set off down Moon Street, staggering slightly as the brandy took effect. He found another bar further up the street, and another one after that. He got into a fight in a third—he wasn't sure what it was about, but he was angry. He nursed his bruises and restored his pride in various other places, but they threw him out of the last one when he ran out of credits for brandy and dope sticks—for real this time. They didn't think it was funny when he tried to tell them about Avrill.

He stood swaying in the street and thought of pawning his father's medallion for more credits. The thought shocked him into panicky sobriety. He'd never been this far out of control before. He headed back toward the hotel, staggering a little but making steady progress. His pupils were dilated and the neon hurt his eyes. He was glad when he entered the band of dimmer territory that surrounded the government district. No one wanted to set up business so close to the constant police patrols.

Chael staggered down the middle of a broad avenue paved with trecherous cobblestones whose uneven surface made navigation difficult. Hearing rustling in the alley just ahead, he stopped and watched. It might have been garbage blowing in the wind, but he saw a shadow flicker too and then hold still.

"Come out!" he brawled, ready to fight again. "Come on out!"

He was tired of wrestling with things he couldn't understand. His subconscious took over. No longer wavering, he fell into a classic defense pose, but the mugger was disinclined to risk the battle. There was another rustle in the alley, a creaking board, and the sound of a quick and stealthy retreat. Disappointed, Chael let his arms drop to his sides. He continued towards his hotel. It was almost dawn.

The door to the Council Chamber slid open, and the Sergeant-at-Arms motioned them in. Jody swallowed nervously. It had taken three days to get even this far. He placed his hopes in Vestra, his mother's sister, the Minister for Security. She faced him across the Chamber. Grey-haired, stern, her green eyes were caught in a net of wrinkles.

"Greetings Councilors," he began. "I am here at the order of my sister, t'Verra Mave, chief trader of Ozine Station." He took a deep breath and faltered suddenly before the unwavering regard of the Council. He wasn't used to making speeches, especially not when so much hung on the outcome. He cleared his throat.

"t'Verra Mave bids me inform you that Ozine Station has been taken by the Dann. Only four of us escaped: my sister and I, t'Verra Lissa, and an outlander named Chael. The rest of our Household is still held by the Dann—if they live."

There was a stir among the Councilors, a murmuring, and a narrowing of eyes. Jody's hopes rose. A short dark-haired woman stood up.

"Honored colleagues, I beg leave to speak." The other voices died away to silence.

"Go ahead, Kestain," the President said.

Kestain bowed slightly. "We are shocked," she began, "by this wrong. But we must not let it force us into over-hasty action. True, we could concentrate our forces, gather the fleet, and strike back at these marauders. But think of the cost! The Dann are powerful, with a rich planetary base. Dare we risk our full force against them? If we lose, it will mean the end of our people. We are not equipped for war." She paused, looking around the Chamber. One or two heads nodded in agreement.

"If we don't act now, we'll be committing suicide!" Jody burst out. "Don't you see, they've taken Ozine Station and with that technology under their control, no one will be able to stand against the Dann."

"Spoken like a man," Kestain said. "All emotion and no prudence. If this matter is so grave, why didn't t'Verra Mave appear before the Council herself?"

"She went to seek help elsewhere," the Wolf witch said scathingly. "She is brave, and she knows better than to rely on a group of old women who are too cowardly to stir their bones."

"Silence!" the President ordered.

Appalled, Jody turned to the Wolf-witch.

12

"Chael! Where have you been? The Chancellor's secretary called and . . . ." Mave stopped abruptly as he came into full view. The sun rose and filled the room with light. He went to the window and pressed the polarizer. It helped some, but not enough. A hot wire of pain rose from the back of his neck to his skull—a warning of things to come.

"What's happened to you?" Mave demanded.

"Had a little fight," he answered, his swollen lip muffling the words. Coming closer, she examined him critically.

"In here," she said finally, pulling him towards the bathroom. Chael spent the next half hour under a cold shower, then sat wrapped in a soggy towel while Mave tended his dishonorable wounds.

"Give me damitiron!" he begged. His head felt ready to blow apart, and his stomach twisted.

"Not on top of what you took last night," she told him coldly. "God knows what the mix would do." She filled up his cup of caff again. "Drink this. We've got to be at the Chancellor's palace in half an hour."

"What!" He stopped with the cup halfway to his lips.

"I finally made contact," she said. "We should be through to the Regent by noon."

"But how?" he asked. The Chancellor had named an impossibly large bribe.

"I sold one of my ships," she said, turning away so he couldn't see her face.

"Mave, no!"

She shrugged. "It's done, Chael. It's too late to

change it. Anyway, what value is a ship when my Household is in danger?"

He had no answer for her, but he was appalled at the price she'd paid. He was still numb with outrage when they reached the Chancellor's palace. An effeminate young secretary led them to the inner office. He bowed—not quite deeply enough—and left them outside the door. Presumably, they were to wait until his Excellency deigned to see them. Chael waited five minutes. He slid back the door and walked in. Mave hesitated a moment, then followed him.

His Excellency was looking in the mirror, fumbling for something caught on a back molar. He glanced up in surprise, fingers still in his mouth. He removed them quickly.

"What are you doing in here?!"

"We're here for our appointment," Chael answered cooly. He moved closer to the desk but didn't sit down. He wanted to be able to reach the Chancellor in a hurry if he had to.

"I didn't call for you. Get out!" His Excellency made shooing motions with his pudgy hands. Chael noticed the nails were painted pale pink.

"Our appointment was for the tenth hour," Chael said. He glanced at a gold chrono set into the pale grey wall. "It's half past that now."

"I'll see you when I'm ready," his Excellency blustered, "and that will probably be never."

Chael advanced a step closer, his hands slowly clenching and unclenching. "You were paid," he said.

His Excellency turned from ripe plum to pale mauve. He seemed unable to look away from the steel cables of Chael's metal hand. Slowly, he edged toward the corner of his desk.

"That was only partial payment," he began.

"Partial payment!" Chael exploded. "A five-ton cargo ship!" His metal hand slammed down on the desk, breaking off a sizeable chunk of opalescent plastic.

His Excellency reached for the panic button set into the corner of his desk, but Chael was faster. His hand slapped on the official's pudgy fingers, and the Chancellor emitted a squeal of pain. He tried to slide out of his chair, and Chael pounced, gathering a fist full of perfumed beard. It came off in his hand, and he fell backward, off balance. The Chancellor raced for the door.

Without rising from her chair, Mave put out one long leg and tripped him. He went down with a thud that rattled the windows. Chael picked him up by the scruff of the neck and slammed him against the wall two or three times for good measure.

"That will do," Mave said. "We still need him to get us through to the Regent."

Reluctantly, Chael dropped the man into the nearest purple plush chair. His Excellency seemed groggy, so he found a carved crystal pitcher of water, and emptied it over his head. The Chancellor sputtered and stirred. One hand went automatically to his chin.

"My beard!"

"It's over by your desk," Mave told him. "You can put it back on later."

He ignored her. "I must have it," he cried frantically. He struggled to his feet and took a couple of wobbly steps toward the beard, but Chael was there before him. He snatched up the facepiece and held it out of his Excellency's reach.

"After you take us to the Regent," he said.

"No!"

"Yes," affirmed Mave. "Quit stalling."

Unwillingly, his Excellency turned to the com-screen.

"He'll see me!" he wailed.

"Leave off the visual," Mave suggested. "Tell him the system is down."

"This is most irregular," the Chancellor muttered, as he punched in the call. It took some time. The Chancellor called his secretary, who called the Regent's palace and was handed through a series of royal undersecretaries. Chael sighed and fidgeted with his Excellency's beard. The Chancellor glanced anxiously at him, and he quit. Then the Senior Secretary was on the line. After some acid comments from that august personage, the Chancellor finally obtained an appointment for them at the fourth hour of that very day.

"This had better be important," the Senior Secretary said. "You're interrupting the Regent's afternoon chess game."

"Of course it's important, you impertinent fool," his Excellency blustered. He shut off the com.

"Now give me my beard and get out. You've got just time enough to get there, if you hurry."

"Not so fast," Chael said. He didn't trust the Chancellor alone with a com-unit. With his beard back on, there was no telling what trouble he'd cause them.

"We could get there on time in your ship," Mave said thoughtfully.

"No. I refuse," the Chancellor said angrily. "You're not taking my ship."

Mave grinned wickedly. "No, your excellency. You are."

They had to let him put his beard on, before he agreed to call for his ship, but a menacing glance from Chael was enough to keep him in line. They rode to the Regent's Palace in stiff, distrustful silence. The marble entrance was manned by a brace of guards, but they parted at a single wave of his Excellency's pudgy hand. They mounted the steps with all deliberate speed, and the performance was repeated another half-a-dozen times before they reached the Regent's chambers. Chael was glad they'd brought his Excellency along, no matter what trouble he might cause them once they were well inside. The massive doors, twice the height of a man, swung back with ponderous dignity, and they followed the Chancellor inside.

The long hall ahead of them seemed empty at first. Carved pillars lined the walls, interspersed with intricately pleated green velvet drapes and gilded mirrors. Clusters of dark, ornate furniture looked lost on the polished floor. Then Chael saw movement at the far end of the room, near the big arched windows. Two men sat over a chess board. With quick angry steps, his Excellency led them toward Prince Graff dall Fall, Regent of Shadriss.

"Your majesty," the Chancellor said, bowing depply, still panting from the speed of his walk. "Please forgive this intrusion. I would never have dreamed of interrupting you, never. I was . . . ."

"Get on with it," the Regent ordered curtly. He was a slender, muscular man in late middle age. His pale grey eyes matched the grey streaks in his beard. His chess companion tapped his piece impatiently against his chair arm. The Chancellor went pale.

"I was forced here, your majesty, forced! I've been beaten, abused—in my own office. These two kidnapped me and made me bring them to you." He flung an accusing hand at Chael and Mave. Jewels glittered on his stubby fingers.

Chael made a move to grab the Chancellor, but halted when he saw the row of blasters pointed at him. A handful of bodyguards had stepped out of concealed alcoves. Chael had no doubt that they'd shoot to kill. They'd lost after all.

"I would never have troubled your majesty if my life were not in danger," the Chancellor whined.

The Regent's chess partner emitted a snort worthy of a cavi. "Your life!" he said, glowering at the hapless Chancellor. "Man, have you rotted your brains with those vile concoctions you drink? How dare you bring assassins into the presence of the Regent!"

"We're not . . . ," Chael began hotly, and the guards moved in, but the Regent intervened.

"Leave him be," he commanded. "I'm curious to hear more about this incident."

"Graff, you can't risk it. Kill them now and ask questions later," the other man said.

"Harlan, you worry too much," his majesty replied. "If these are assassins, they've been unnaturally slow in getting to the point of their visit." He turned to the Chancellor. "Now, what was it you claim they did to you?"

His excellency took a shaky breath and plunged into an incoherent diatribe. "Tortured me, beaten, destroyed my office, no respect, thieves." He had to stop suddenly to catch his breath. Mave's voice rang out clearly in the pause.

"Chael stole his beard."

The Regent's lips twitched in what might have been a smile in a warmer man. Lord Harlan gave a short bark of laughter. The Chancellor stood with his mouth open, too dismayed to even glare at the chief trader.

"Well, did he?" the Regent asked.

The Chancellor swallowed and nodded. "But that was just one among many abuses. It's not fitting that a man in my position . . . ."

"I think perhaps that was the 'torture' that counted, though, eh?" said his majesty.

The Chancellor grew purple. "I tell you, it's not fitting . . . ."

"You'll tell me nothing," the Regent snapped. "You forget to whom you speak."

Lord Harlan's dagger was out of its sheath, and the Chancellor trembled, sweating like a man in a fever dream. Chael almost felt sorry for the little man until he remembered the size of the bribe Mave had paid.

"You may go," the Regent said.

"But your majesty," his Excellency began.

"You may go. I should hate to be forced to find a new Chancellor."

His Excellency backed out, bowing deeply and still trembling.

The Regent turned to Mave. "Now," he said, "tell me why you're here." Lord Harlan sighed and put away his dagger. The chess game seemed forgotten.

"The Dann have taken Ozine Station," Mave answered promptly. "They propose to control the Ozine, and through them, to control the League. Shadriss will be one of the first to feel the effect."

"Why should I believe you?" the Regent asked casually, leaning back in his chair. Lord Harlan, however, appeared interested at last.

"Why would I waste my time with your officials, if it were not so?" Mave replied scathingly. "It's cost me enough to see you. My Household is being held hostage by the Dann even now—if they still live."

Prince Graff considered for a moment. "It is true," he said, "that the traders are not given to fraud, as are the rest of us poor mortals." He smiled slightly. Chael remembered Lissa and was silent.

"The safety of your Household is of no concern of ours," Lord Harlan said. "How does controlling Ozine Station make them a threat to us? The Ozine won't fight, and the Dann have never been a match for Shadriss.''

"The Ozine won't fight," Mave conceded. "But their technology can be used for war, and the Dann know it.''

"Well, trader," the Regent said, "we can see if your story fits what facts we have. Your name and Household?''

"t'Verra Mave," she answered.

Prince Graff raised one aristocratic eyebrow. ''The resident trader of Ozine Station?''

She nodded.

"So then, we can assume you know what you're talking about," he said thoughtfully. "And this one with you?'' He gestured toward Chael.

"An assistant. I'm considering accepting him into my Household," she said, bending the truth. At least it gave Chael a better status than mere hanger-on.

"Very well," the Regeent said. His arms came down and, decisively, he flipped on the com and spoke to his secretary. "Send me our latest information on Ozine Station, and make sure you indicate when it came in.'' He turned away from the screen and regarded them keenly.

"There's no point in being uncivilized while we wait," he said. "Will you join us in a glass of our local brandy?''

"Who are you?" the President demanded. White-haired and erect, she dominated the Council Chamber. Even Ona grew respectful.

"I am Ona, the Wolf-witch," she answered. "My people are warriors. We fight for our land and our honor. The trader Mave has endured many hardships and even betrayal in her struggle to free her House-

135

hold. It is not fitting that you, the leaders of her people, should abandon her.''

There was silence afterward as the Councilors mulled her words. Then Vestra rose to speak.

''What this girl says is true,'' she began. ''My niece was betrayed by a member of her Household. t'Verra Lissa turned against her, but the renegade was struck down in turn by this girl who calls herself Wolf-witch. Mave is now on Shadriss, trying to recruit help from the League. But we all know how slow the League is to move. They are too careful of their own interests, even as some traders would have us be.'' Here she glanced scornfully at Kestain. ''Councilors, I move that we give all possible aid. t'Verra Mave's call for help touches our deepest values. If we fail to fight for what we believe in, then we are nothing, and we deserve the destruction the Dann will bring.''
the Dann will bring.''

The Regent's brandy was nothing like the acid poison Chael had drunk the night before. He sipped it slowly, savoring the rich taste and wondering if he'd live long enough to afford a whole bottle of his own. The com-screen buzzed, interrupting his speculations.

''Your majesty,'' the Senior Secretary announced, ''there have been no ships from Ozine Station reported on Shadriss for the past month.'' The Secretary shuffled a handful of forms. ''Administrator Coribund asked about it just last week. It seems that we're getting dangerously low on certain chemical supplies. At last word, Ozine Station had suffered two minor attacks from the Dann.''

''Thank you. That will do.'' The Regent snapped off the screen, and his fingers formed a steeple. ''So it is true. Very well, we must plan our countermove.''

The planning went on for the rest of the day, as the Regent and Lord Harlan argued tactics with Mave.

Her efforts were to save her Household, theirs to destroy the Dann. Chael grew bored with the talk of ships and people who were only names to him, and his thoughts wandered to the treasures of Ozine Home.

"Of course I'm right," Ona said, overriding Jody's protest. *"What more can we do here? Your leaders finally have seen reason. Your fleet is preparing, but it will be days before they arrive at Ozine Station. Vestra said so herself."*

"But going there on our own won't help the Household!" Jody insisted.

"We'll get the Ozine to fight the invaders," she countered.

"The Ozine don't fight!"

"Nonsense. Everyone fights when her home is threatened."

"Not the Ozine," Jody said, but she wouldn't listen. The way of the Ozine was beyond her experience. He couldn't stop her. Jody knew the Wolf-witch was craftier than he, and once she had determined to go to Ozine Station, there was no way he could bar her.

The best he could do was go along to ease her way. He'd grown disproportionately fond of this stubborn barbarian female, and he didn't want to lose her to the Dann. Ignoring his misgivings, he agreed to be her pilot.

13

During the next few days, Chael had no time to dream of treasure. All his hours were taken up in a multitude of preparations for the forthcoming battle, for battle it would be. The Regent had cast his lot with the traders at last. The fleet of Shadriss made ready to oust the Dann from Ozine Station. And there was their own ship to prepare, or rather Mave's ship. The Regent had given her the War Hound when he found out the size of the bribe paid to the Chancellor. Not so large as the lost freighter, she was a Class-1 cruiser, able to outrun any ship made.

It seemed to Chael that the Regent finally realized the importance of keeping Ozine Station securely within the League's protection. The League was a vast sprawl of thousands of worlds, and it existed not so much as a government as an agreement of honor. Under the League, there was peace and commerce between worlds. The Dann would end all that in a bloody war of conquest.

Shadrissport looked ill-prepared for death, he thought as he edged past a fat merchant. He was headed for the outfitter's, where the working clothes they'd ordered yesterday should be ready. It was a clear dry morning, as days so often were in this place. He'd been in the city so long now that he scarcely noticed the stench from the river Ur and the reek of unwashed bodies. As he neared the outfitter's, the crowd thinned, and Chael quickened his pace. His change of speed threw off the aim of the marksman, and the blaster bolt intended for his head blackened the plaster wall a step behind him. He was down and rolling before his ears were even sure of the sound.

He scanned the suddenly deserted street. The bolt had come from above and on the other side of the way, but there was no betraying movement at any of the upper windows. Then the flash of sunlight on the blaster barrel warned him. The would-be assassin was on the roof, and Chael's cover was no cover at all. The barrel was aimed right at his back. He scrambled for an open doorway, just as a second bolt seared the ground where he'd been.

Once inside, he crouched out of sight in the shadows. He couldn't see the marksman now, but Chael was sure he was still out there, waiting. The only weapon Chael carried was his knife. He had no chance against a blaster. This was a time to retreat, to find out who was out to crisp his hide and why. Then he'd act. He looked around the hallway that sheltered him.

The broken door stood ajar. It had been a long, long time since anyone had tried to close the ruined portal. The wind blew more trash in, adding to the hoard of debris against the stairs. Yet the building wasn't deserted. Chael heard voices and music. Somewhere a woman called, and he smelled bread baking. The short hall behind him ended in a blank wall. He heard people moving behind the closed doors on either side, the occupants oblivious to his peril.

Softly, Chael climbed the first flight of stairs. The second floor offered no more chance of escape than the first. He climbed again, hoping for a way to the roof. But the stairs ended at the blank third-floor passage. Chael swore once, then stood listening. He heard voices in the apartment on his right, but no sound came from behind the door to his left. Below him, he heard the muffled scrape of footsteps on the stairs.

That decided him; no one but the assassin would

need to walk so stealthily. His knife was already in his right hand. He slipped the blade in between the jamb and the frame and forced open the lock. The bolt yielded easily to his metal hand. Quietly, Chael stepped into the shuttered apartment. He closed the door gently behind him and stood still a moment, letting his eyes adjust. He heard the sound of soft breathing, and someone stirred sleepily in the bed. Chael stiffened.

"So, it's the gallant outlander again," Avrill said. He yawned and stretched gracefully. "What brings you to my door at this early hour of the day?"

It took only a moment to place that elegant drawl—the boy at the bar. His cheeks flushed at the memory. The hour was well past noon, but Chael wasn't prepared to quibble. Avrill's days and nights no doubt ran different from the norm. He willed the furious pace of his heartbeat to slow.

"I didn't know it was your door," Chael said awkwardly. "I'm looking for a way out of the building."

"The exit is at the foot of the stairs." Avrill seemed put out that Chael had come to see him only by accident.

"There's also a man with a blaster waiting there."

Avrill shrugged and began combing his long dark hair. Chael knew he needed the boy's help.

"I'm glad to see you, Avrill," he said. That was true enough. He'd rather face Avrill than some outraged householder. "But I didn't know you lived here." Quickly, he explained about the sniper on the roof.

"And you think he's out in the hall now?" Avrill asked, his brown eyes huge.

"Probably." Chael didn't want to panic the boy. But he'd misjudged Avrill again.

His smile was dazzling. "Outlander, I forgive you

for your lack of tact. I haven't seen such excitement since first we met.''

"It's not a game, Avrill." Chael was annoyed. "He shot to kill."

"But you escaped. Now, we'll see that you continue in your good fortune." Naked, Avrill got up and walked over to peer out between the shutters. "The street's back to normal," he said, turning to Chael. "You say you don't know why he tried to burn you?"

Chael shook his head no.

"Then I think you'd better stay here while I find out," Avrill said decisively. He began pulling on his clothes.

"Don't answer the door," he warned. "If anyone seems determined to enter," He crossed to a large cupboard. "there's a hiding place here." He pressed the wall next to the cupboard, and a pannel slid aside. "There's a peephole, so you can see out, but don't make any noise. It's not soundproof." He closed the pannel and reached into the cupboard for a black velvet cloak.

"Thank you, Avrill."

"Thank you, outlander." He smiled again, and Chael was surprised to see that the boy really was enjoying himself. "There's food and something to drink over there," Avrill said, nodding toward a carved chest in the corner. He swirled the cloak around him and was gone, leaving Chael to listen carefully for the sound of footsteps in the hall.

Some of the Household waited passively for death, but that had never been Sandar's way. Grey-haired, grey-eyed, he was Vestra's first husband and had joined Mave's Household temporarily to help set up a new trade contract. Sandar was fond of his wife's niece, and the Dann treachery angered him more than

141

he let show. The years had added a wily quality to his courage, and now he searched with all his skill for a way to defeat the Dann.

It wasn't easy. The Dann controlled the landing field, and the Ozine would offer no help. Yet to leave the Station in Dann hands meant death for them all. All the trader Households, and the League worlds as well, were in danger. Yet again his eyes scanned the room. They were kept prisoner in their old quarters. A force screen blocked the only entry hall and sealed them off from the control room. There were only fifteen members of the Household left alive—fifteen out of thirty. They looked lost in the once busy dayroom.

Sandar looked and saw no means of escape. The cool breeze that blew over his shoulders was too familiar to be noticed.

In their hotel suite on Shadriss, Mave waited impatiently for Chael to return. What was keeping him? The com-screen buzzed, and she rushed to answer it.

"Yes?"

"Chief Trader t'Verra Mave?"

She nodded impatiently. The caller appeared to be checking her image against some identity form. At last, he seemed satisfied.

"I have a private message for you from Shadriss med-center."

"Spit it out!"

The messenger frowned distastefully. He'd hoped the trader would make things easy for him.

"The med-center wishes to notify you that the patient t'Verra Lissa has left the mental rehab department."

"Left?" Mave frowned. "But where did she go?"

The messenger looked embarrassed. "They don't know," he admitted. "She just left—ran away."

"But she couldn't have!"

Chael heard the latch click and quickly slipped into the hidden recess. It was dark and stuffy inside, but it offered shelter of a sort. He remembered the peephole and looked out. Avrill was dropping his velvet cape over the back of a chair.

"You can come out now, outlander. Although you're not safe a step outside this room."

"So I gathered," Chael said, leaving his hiding place.

Avrill threw himself down on the unmade bed and regarded Chael with interest.

"Did you find out anything?" Chael asked.

"Oh yes," Avrill said, playing with his dark curls. "There are plenty of stories going around about that metal hand of yours, but mostly they talk about the enormous number of credits offered for your life."

"For my life?!"

"Yes." He nodded admiringly. "For you dead, and for the chief trader alive. I suppose he plans to make her end more entertaining."

"Who does?" Chael asked angrily. Fear for Mave filled him, and he glared at the boy who took it all so lightheartedly.

"The Chancellor, of course," Avrill replied matter-of-factly. "The story of the Chancellor's beard is all over the city. He'll have to kill you both if he wants to appear in public again. It seems he holds this woman more to blame than you." He glanced shrewdly at Chael. "She means a lot to you, eh?"

"No. It's just . . . ." He stopped. "I suppose she does."

"Well, if you take my advice, you'll both get off planet as fast as you can lift. The Chancellor's offering a very tempting sum. Very tempting," he added, "even for news of your whereabouts."

Cheal looked at him, and Avrill looked back in round-eyed innocence.

"Avrill, you haven't."

"Not yet," the boy admitted. "But seven thousand credits will go a long way. And poor old sa'Raster hasn't been the same since you beat him to a pudding. How am I supposed to live without my best client?"

"I was only trying to help," Chael said.

"I know. That's why I don't hold it against you—even if you did cost me a bundle of credits. No one's ever tried to help me before."

It seemed a sad admission to Chael, and it made him feel more guilty than ever. Than an idea flickered dimly into being.

"Avrill, can you draw me a map of the city?"

In a quiet corner of Shadrissport, Sullat, leader of the Dann, waited for a chance to reach the com-screen unseen. Three clerks were in the office. Soon, two left, headed for the cafeteria. Sullat decided to take a chance on the remaining man.

The clerk never saw the inhumanly swift blow that broke his neck. The body was shoved aside, and the Dann leader dialed a code on a seldom-used frequency. There was only a short delay before Henyab's elongated face appeared.

"What took so long?" the Dann captain demanded. "It's been days since your last transmission. I was afraid something had gone wrong."

"I can take care of myself," Sullat answered brusquely. "I've found out that the chief trader has managed to get League backing. The Regent is sending his fleet against Ozine Station."

"They wouldn't dare damage the Station," Henyab protested. "They need the Ozine."

"*Prince Graff is no fool,*" *said Sullat.* "*He knows what we'll be able to do with Ozine technology under our control. The only thing that stands in the way of the destruction of Ozine Station is the trader Mave's concern for her Household. I expect the Regent will cause her to disappear before the attack. But if we can hold the Station for just a little longer, we can learn enough to make ourselves invulnerable.*"

"*We won't be able to hold out long,*" *the captain said.* "*Not against the whole fleet of Shadriss.*"

Sullat nodded agreement. "*The Regent's fleet must be delayed, and I think I know of a way.*"

Twice a day the force screen was opened for meals to be brought in. The Dann evidently didn't know how to use the Ozine food processor and delivery system. The meals they brought were crude—a sort of bland stew and coarse bread. Sandar suspected that it was typical Dann fare.

He'd discussed his desperate plan with the others, and they'd all agreed it was their only chance. The Household waited, clustered near the sealed hallway. Soon, the screen would be lowered for the evening meal, and they'd make their move. Sandar swallowed. His mouth was dry, but he was determined.

"That's suicide!" Avrill exclaimed.

"Not if you have the ground car waiting for me," said Chael. "All you have to do then is make the call and keep out of sight. When the Chancellor's assassins show up, I'll make my escape and join Mave on the War Hound. You can collect your reward for the information later, when it's safe."

"But there's no guarantee you'll get away. They may block the roads."

Chael was touched by the boy's concern for his

safety. At least he hoped it was for his safety, and not for the even bigger reward offered for his death. Avrill still puzzled him. The boy looked no more than seventeen standard years old, but in some ways he was ancient. Chael never knew whether he was dealing with Avrill the adventurous boy, or Avrill the streetwise prostitute.

"This way I'll at least know where they are," he said, putting a reassuring hand on Avrill's shoulder.

But this time there was no coy glance in return. Avrill looked worried.

"You're trying to distract them while that trader woman gets to the ship, aren't you." It wasn't a question, and Chael didn't deny it.

"You'll never make it. A fast ground car won't be enough. You might get a good start, but they'd trap you before you reached the port. There'll be too many of them, and you don't know the streets well enough. You won't have time to be reading a map."

"I'll make it," Chael said. "Anyway, I'll try."

Avrill frowned in concentration. "If we could confuse them and get you to the port before they realize what's happened—There are some people who owe me favors."

"Avrill, no."

"You don't trust me, do you?" His dark eyes were grave, and he suddenly looked much older.

"I don't know," Chael admitted. He didn't dare offer some comforting lie. He was sure Avrill's experience included lies in every form, and he'd pounce on the first hint of falsehood. Somehow, he'd won the boy's trust. It was such a fragile thing; he meant to keep it at whatever cost to himself. Avrill stood on the brink of an abyss, and Chael was all that held him back. He could push the boy either way—to safety or to destruction.

"I can't know, Avrill, because you don't know if

you can trust yourself. Isn't that so?" Avrill looked ready to run or fight or explode in some terrible, destructive way. Gruffly, Chael punched him on the shoulder.

"Still, a man's got to trust his friends. Without them, what's he got? So I guess I do trust you."

Avrill smiled suddenly, looking like a boy again, and Chael went on. "But this is dangerous. It's not a game. You understand?"

"Of course," Avrill said, but this time Chael felt sure he meant it.

Jody brought the ship down in a crater well away from the landing field. The setdown was rough; a glance at the instruments told him they wouldn't rise again without repairs. Calmly, Ona climbed out of her shock harness. He was amazed again by how readily she'd taken to human technology, almost as if she'd been born surrounded by it. He helped her into her suit, and they stepped out. The suits were body-covering overalls with clear faceplates. Less comfortable than the Ozine-made belts, they served the same purpose, and were cheaper to buy and easier to find.

They moved carefully, working their way towards a small maintenance vent. The hard, motionless gleam of stars in vacuum was all around them as they walked over the pale lava of Ozine Station's barren exterior. The surface away from the landing area was rough, and the gravity outside the interior inertia field was less than half standard. The combination made walking dangerous. Ona especially had trouble. Only experience could produce coordination in low gravity. Jody put out an arm to steady her as she stumbled.

"There," he said, pointing to a narrow airlock. "That vent should open into one of the abandoned areas."

"What are you waiting for then?"

The suit's com-unit distorted her voice, but there was no disguising that characteristic impatience. Jody sighed and headed for the vent. The shaft was sealed with a mechanical airlock, instead of the more usual force screens—a fail-safe measure, he supposed. It opened stiffly, requiring some muscle, but it opened. Air hissed in, and the moisture fogged their suits. As soon as the frost melted, Jody opened the inner hatch, and they cautiously entered the interior of Ozine Station.

No one waited for them in the corridor. Jody felt certain that their landing had been detected, but he doubted that the Dann monitored the maintenance hatches. They'd be expected at the main gate. He hoped to be well hidden before anyone realized the truth. Gripping his blaster, he led the way down the hall.

"I've got to get to a com-screen and warn Mave. She's in as much danger as I am, maybe more."

"You won't get ten steps outside that door," Avrill said, blocking his way. "The reward is too high. There's a seven thousand credit price on your life." He threw his hands up in exasperation. "I must be mad to settle for only a tenth of that for turning you in."

Chael stepped around him, and Avrill dodged in front again. They did a crab-wise dance all the way to the door.

"Chael, listen to me. This is my city. I know what will happen." Avrill's slender hands dropped onto Chael's shoulders. Chael felt the boy's tension and fear. "Please, please, listen to me."

"I've got to warn her," Chael insisted, realizing that he was as much caught in the habit of duty as the chief trader. "She won't believe anyone else."

"All right," Avrill said, accepting the inevitable. "But at least don't go out there with a sign around your neck saying 'kill me.' "

"What do you mean?"

"You need to disguise yourself," the boy said. "Anyone looking at that shipsuit can spot you for an outlander. You need to look as if you belong here."

He hurried to the closet and began pulling out clothes. Silks and satins were thrown in a careless pile on the floor.

"Here," he said, holding up a tunic and trousers of brilliant orange. "I think these might fit you. They're too big for me."

Chael eyed the flame-colored garments dubiously. Still, Avrill's choice was probably right. His own rather ordinary face would never be noticed above that costume.

Reluctantly, Chael peeled off his kanin velvet and pulled on the orange outfit. It was a tight squeeze. The clothes may have been too big for Avrill, but they fit Chael like a second skin. The tunic had long sleeves, but the front opened in a vee that nearly reached his navel. The pants were long enough, but seemed dangerously close to splitting. He put his own black boots on again. Avrill's were much too small. A cape of vertical orange and black stripes and a wide black hat with a plume completed the picture.

Chael looked in the mirror and was startled by the gaudy dandy that confronted him. He repressed an urge to laugh. He could tell that Avrill thought he looked very fine. He slipped his father's medallion into a pocket of the tunic. He might not approve of his new finery, but he had to admit that he looked utterly unlike himself.

"It is a little bright," Avrill conceded. "But no one's going to guess that there's an outlander under those clothes."

They reached a public com-screen without trouble. One or two bare-breasted women favored them with smiles, but no one seemed inclined to call the Chancellor's men.

"You keep watch," Chael said, as he fed credits into the com.

"All right. But hurry up." Avrill leaned against the side of the screen, cleaning his nails with a silver-handled dagger. His body partially hid Chael and kept any passerby from having a view of the screen. It took only a moment to reach Mave.

"Chael!?" She seemed to be staring at his hat. It took a moment to remember the new clothes.

"It's a disguise," he explained. "The Chancellor's put up a seven thousand credit reward for my life—and for you too."

"He wouldn't dare!"

"He has. There's been one near-miss already. Mave, listen to me. There's no time to talk. I want you to get aboard the War Hound and stay there. You understand? Go now, as quickly as you can. Seal the hatch and don't let anyone aboard."

"But what about you?" Her green eyes were large and anxious.

"I'll meet you there as soon as I can. I've got help and a plan." He didn't like to think of how fragile that plan was. "Just get to the ship. You'll be safe there. Hurry, they could come for you anytime."

"All right. I'll wait for you on the War Hound." She paused. "Please be careful, Chael."

The screen went blank. Chael turned to Avrill.

"All right," he said. "It's time to call your friends."

Mave turned away from the com-screen, worried but glad that now she could act rather than wait helplessly. She opened the closet and glanced at the clothes inside. Better just to leave them, she thought. Chael had said time was short, and he always meant what he said.

She snapped the closet shut and turned to the small safe set in the wall. Her palm on the lock opened it. She took out the stack of credits and thrust them into her belt pouch.

According to the room meter, they still had another seven hours rent paid on their suite. She decided not to press the check-out for a refund. If the Chancellor's men came and found their clothes here and time on the meter, they might think she'd return. She drew out twenty credits from her belt and fed the money into the slot. It added twelve hours to their time. Satisfied, she drew on her cloak and went out, slapping the lock plate behind her.

When she stepped out into the street, the sky was already red and purple with dusk. There were no ground cars in sight. Well, so much the better, she thought. No one could be trusted—not with such a reward offered. She wondered if Lissa wandered somewhere in this dim and heavily scented twilight. She'd had no chance to tell Chael that Lissa was missing. She glanced again up and down the street. Then pulling her hood more tightly to hide her face, she started towards the landing field. Behind her, two men rose from the sidewalk table and followed. A tall, slender figure hesitated in a darkened doorway for a moment, then Sullat followed too.

Gong by little-used ways, Jody and Ona worked their way closer to the stim vats. The vats were the heart of the Station, and there they would find the

Ozine. The control room and the landing field had been given over to the traders, and now were in Dann hands. But stim formed the heart of Ozine society. The use of stim and the visions it caused governed every aspect of their lives. His sister had avoided the stim vats. To her, they represented near-death and the reason for her long bondage at the Station. Because of her participation in the experiment with stim, she was the one chosen to guard the Ozine, and there was no end to that duty. But Jody had no such weight on his spirit, and he'd spent much of his time studying the Ozine and their culture. One thing he had learned—without stim, there would be no Ozine.

He pulled Ona back against the wall as two Dann went by—both thin, one tall, the other short; neither looked around. Silently, he motioned for her to follow him. Behind the vats were the living quarters for the stim-tenders. There, they'd find the Ozine. After that—he glanced at Ona—who could tell?

"I think you should take care of it yourself," Lord Harlan told the Regent. "The Chancellor is a bungler."

"Calm yourself, Harlan. If the Chancellor succeeds, we're rid of the traders and can do what we like with the Station. If he fails, we'll go along with the original plan. It won't hurt our status in the League to be known as a champion of the underdog." He smiled. "They may yet bring us another bone."

14

Chael crouched tensely, waiting for Avrill to return. The alley was filthy and so narrow that not even a reflection of moonlight penetrated. Somewhere nearby the river Ur flowed black and oily. There was a rustle of cloth, and a slender shadow stood near him.

"It's all set," Avrill whispered, gently pushing Chael's knife away from his throat. "They'll start as soon as they see us leave."

"Avrill, what will you do with the reward?"

"What will I do with it?" It was too dark to see his face, but Chael could picture the boy's astonishment. "I'll spend it. I'm not going to sit on all those credits."

"You could go a long way with that kind of money. You could get away from here, away from sa'Raster and his kind."

"You don't know what you're talking about," Avrill whispered.

Chael reached out in the darkness—put his arm around the boy's shoulders.

"Avrill, promise me you'll think about it."

"What do you care what I do?" Chael felt him trembling. "What's it to you?"

"I care," Chael said. "Promise me, Avrill."

"All right," Avrill said finally. "I promise to think about it. But that's all!"

"That's all I ask."

The pure white of the force screen faded out, and three Dann stepped into the room. Two were armed guards; one pushed a cart laden with food.

"Now!" Sandar yelled.

They rushed forward. The first guard went down, and the second grabbed the cook as a shield.

Three traders fell as the guard's blaster burned them. Sandar saw the muzzle swing towards him. He threw himself to one side, a blaze of agony on his arm.

The Dann backed away, the first guard stumbling. Then they were out, and the impenetrable white force screen faded back into being. The rebellion was a failure. They had three more dead—for nothing. Sandar closed his eyes and gave in to the pain.

Sullat watched the two who trailed Mave, wondering who had sent them. They obviously meant the chief trader no good. The woman was headed towards the ship, and that fit in with Sullat's own plans. But first, these two must be disposed of before they interfered. Silently, the Dann leader moved in for the kill.

It was a cheap bar, not much different from the one where he'd first met Avrill. Chael pretended to drink from his glass of racheff. Why had the Regent allowed this hunt? he wondered. Did Prince Graff even know of it, or was his majesty playing games of his own? He put the speculation aside as Avrill entered.

The boy walked slowly past him. He glanced casually at Chael, then looked more sharply and moved on. Chael pretended not to notice. They'd already agreed on their roles.

From the corner of his eye, he saw Avrill go to a com-screen. Chael stared into his glass, obviously not interested. Avrill left the screen and sat down at a table near the door. Chael looked at him, as if noticing the boy for the first time. Avrill's hand went to his collar, and he pushed his skullcap forward, as if vainly trying to hide his face.

Two or three of the other customers had noticed the byplay. That was good. Avrill would need witnesses to prove that he'd really spotted Chael. Chael had cost

Avrill his best customer. The Chancellor should have no trouble believing that Avrill would spot the outlander and turn him in for the reward.

Sure of his audience, Chael let his eyes narrow thoughtfully as he stared at the boy. He was worried—afraid Avrill would be caught, afraid Mave wouldn't make it to the ship—and he let that feeling show on his face. Abruptly, Chael pushed away his drink and started for the door. Avrill half-rose, then dropped back into his seat.

Breathlessly, Mave ran up the ramp to the War Hound. There'd been sounds of a scuffle behind her at the gate, but she wasted no time investigating. The lock yielded to her palm pressure, and she hurried in.

For just a moment, her back was to the open hatch, and that was long enough for Sullat. With speed no human could match, she entered the ship, hiding just beyond the storage lockers.

Startled, Mave turned. She'd seen something flicker—She blinked and shook her head. She was tired and nervous, and her eyes were playing tricks on her. She shut the hatch and locked it.

Chael sat on the passenger side of the ground car, and Avrill slid in behind the wheel.

"Well?"

"I think they bought it," Avrill said.

The car started easily, and they moved quickly away from the bar. Nearby, Chael heard another ground car start up and another and another. Avrill had called in all his favors tonight. Half-a-dozen men matching Chael's description were moving away from the waterfront bar.

They drove beside the river and for a time, the street seemed deserted. Then the false peace was shattered by a roar and blaze of light, as another ground car streaked by. Hastily, Chael drew Avrill's black cloak over him. The plumed hat was already on the floor. Avrill pulled into an alley.

"Up this way," the boy said, rapidly climbing a flight of rickety stairs to the roof. Chael followed. Below him, he saw the bright flare of blasters, and two orange-clad figures separated, moving away in different directions. How much of the reward money had Avrill promised to his decoys? he wondered.

The roof was bare and windswept, cooler and cleaner than the city streets. A small flitter sat waiting for them. They scrambled in, and Avrill threw the controls to lift.

The machine moved quickly and silently, but Chael doubted they'd make it all the way to the landing field before they were spotted. With luck, they might get close. For an hour, they floated above the city, and he was almost relaxed, until suddenly there was a whine of engines in the night, and a laser flared, sending drops of molten metal spraying across Chael's lap. The flitter jerked, canting to one side. They'd lost an impeller. A dark shape flashed by, showing only by the reflection of their own lights.

Avrill cut their lights and struggled desperately with the remaining impeller. They were falling fast, at an acute angle, and he had to put them down near the port, or they'd both die tonight. The lasers flashed again, firing at their silhouette against the stars. The second impeller cut out, and they fell the last thirty meters in freefall.

Chael heard the crash and the ugly sound of tearing metal and plastic, as he slammed against the shock harness and then back against the seat. Dimmly, he heard Avrill calling his name and felt the boy pulling him free of the harness. Chael half-fell from his seat, and Avrill staggered under his weight.

"Walk!" the boy said, gasping.

The outlander was even heavier than he looked. They had only seconds before the Chancellor's men closed in.

Leaning heavily on Avrill, Chael stumbled away from the wreckage. By the time they reached the perimeter fence surrounding the landing field, he was able to walk unaided. Avrill dragged him into the shadow of a loader left parked against the fence.

"Where's your ship?" he hissed, crouching next to Chael.

Chael turned and looked over the landing field. It took an effort to focus his eyes.

"There," he said, pointing to the cruiser that perched dark and lean on tripod legs. "The War Hound."

There was more than fifty meters of lighted open ground between them and the ship. Chael heard voices near where they'd crashed. The Chancellor's men were closing in.

"It's no good, Avrill. They'll spot us any minute. Get out of here while you still can." He felt dizzy and clutched the loader for support.

Avrill ignored him. He was studying the fence.

"Go," Chael urged.

"I'll go all right," Avrill said, turning to look at him. "But first, you're going over that fence. I can distract the Chancellor's men long enough for you to reach the ship."

"No. It's too dangerous."

"Look," Avrill said, growing angry, "we do it my way, or we don't do it at all. Do you want to sit here until they come for us?"

"No. But—"

"All right. So first we get you over the fence." He

157

looked up at the loader that sheltered them. "Do you think you can climb on top of this without making a racket?"

"It looks like I'll have to," Chael said.

The loader reached nearly to the top of the fence. It was poor security to leave it parked so close, but entirely typical of Shadrissport.

Chael stifled a groan as he got to his feet. His right leg was stiff and throbbed with pain when he put his weight on it, but he didn't think it was broken. Sticky blood smeared his face and hands, and he had a lump on the back of his head where he'd slammed against the seat. He couldn't see well, but it did seem as though Avrill had come off more lightly. The boy climbed agilely onto the loader.

"Come on," he urged Chael. "I'll help you up."

It was a painful, desperate climb. At every moment, Chael expected to feel the sear of a blaster bolt. He was breathing in hoarse gasps when he finally reached the top of the fence, and sweat ran down his face and back. He heard the sound of voices coming nearer.

"Drop over and wait," Avrill said. "I'll go off a ways and make enough noise to draw them."

Chael leaned towards the boy and took Avrill's hand in his own good hand.

"Thank you, Avrill." He wished Avrill could come away with them, but he knew he had nothing to offer but more danger. Even if they tried to reach the ship together, they'd be spotted as soon as they were on open ground.

"Remember your promise," Chael said finally.

"I'll remember." Avrill's free hand gripped his arm with surprising strength. "Goodbye, my friend."

With Avrill's help, Chael dropped to the other side of the fence. The shadows stirred, and the boy was gone. Chael waited, feeling lonely and exposed. The night breeze was cool and damp. He shivered.

"Look out! There he goes!" someone shouted. Chael pressed against the fence, but the voices were moving away from him. He heard a ringing metallic crash, and a scream from one of the men.

"Catch him! He's getting away!"

Chael waited no longer. Avrill's ruse had worked. He headed for the ship, hobbling painfully on his stiff leg. The sounds of the chase behind him grew fainter. Then he was on the ramp of the War Hound. His hand hit the entry buzzer, and he leaned against the hatch.

It opened suddenly, and he fell into Mave's arms.

Silently, Sullat watched the arrival of the outlander. She remained in hiding, wanting the ship off the ground before she made her move. The chief trader locked the hatch and dragged the man to one of the bunks. She found a small med-kit and began tending his injuries.

"I say we're better off in orbit."

"But Chael, I'm sure the Regent doesn't know about this. The Chancellor must be acting on his own." Mave looked fine-drawn with worry.

"It's the Chancellor's doing, all right. I'm not arguing with that." He shifted his bruised leg to a more comfortable position. If only his head would stop aching . . . .

"I think the Regent knows what's going on," he said. "The Chancellor couldn't set up a hunt like that without Prince Graff hearing about it, and that means he condones it. Until the Regent's fleet is ready, we'll be safer in orbit where we can run if we have to."

"All right," Mave said at last. "Maybe you're right. I'll take the ship up."

She turned to enter their course in the navigator, and Chael closed his eyes. He wondered if Avrill had escaped. Someday, he'd come back and find out. He'd make sure Avrill got off-planet and into a better life—if either of them lived that long.

"The course is set," Mave said. Chael opened his eyes. "Are you sure you can take lift-off?" she asked.

"I'll be okay."

He forced his thoughts away from Avrill and considered again the problem of the Regent's involvement. They'd agreed on a plan of action only after much debate. He and Mave would leave six hours ahead of the fleet. In that six-hour lead time, they'd take the War Hound in at max speed and do what they could to rescue the Household. It was a flimsy plan, but they had a chance—a very slim chance—of success. But it also meant that the Dann would be on the alert when the Regent's ships arrived. Prince Graff would lose his edge; his casualties would be higher. But if he and Mave never arrived? Chael could almost hear Lord Harlan urging the safer course: let the Chancellor have them, and we'll have Ozine Station.

"We're cleared for lift-off," said Mave, interrupting his thoughts. "Not even the Chancellor can tamper with the port control system."

"I'm ready," Chael said. He stretched out flat on his back on the bunk. The pressure built slowly, unbearably, and he heard himself groan.

"Jody. We thought you were dead," Katt said.

The Ozine Leader sounded neither surprised nor excited at the sudden reappearance. That was what Jody had expected. He knew that, if he asked, Katt would tell him he'd forseen it all. Privately, Jody doubted the validity of many of the Ozine predictions. The stim-induced visions seemed too sketchy to deserve much faith. That being so, he'd better explain himself.

"My sister and I escaped from the Dann," he told Katt, "along with the outlander and another of our Household. Mave has gone to get help from the League, and Ona and I have come to do what we can here."

Ona decided to speak, even though he'd warned her to wait.

"We've come to help you fight the Dann," she said, stepping forward. "To kill them and reclaim your territory."

"Ona," Jody began impatiently, "the Ozine don't fight!"

He stopped abruptly when he saw Katt's face. The Ozine Leader was flushed, his mouth and eyes narrowed in his people's expression of astonishment. Jody had never seen so much display of emotion by an adult Ozine.

"Oh, joyous day!" Katt cried at last. "It is she. The Regenetrix has come!"

Ona was annoyed by the interruption.

"What are you talking about, old man?" she demanded, but Katt didn't notice the lack of respect.

"You are the Regenetrix, savior of the Ozine. The first female of our species for three hundred years." He took her arm and tried to tug her towards the door.

"You must see the medics at once," he commanded.

"Keep your hands off me!" Ona said, tearing free. She was far stronger than Katt, and she didn't like this odd behavior. It didn't fit in with her plans for war. At last, Jody recovered from his astonishment enough to speak up.

"This woman is from a barbarian planet on the far side of nowhere. She can't be your Regenetrix!"

"She is," Katt insisted. "I have forseen it."

He reached for Ona again, and she showed him

away. He hit the wall, and she kicked him viciously in the stomach. Katt doubled over and lay moaning on the floor.

"Now we're in for it," Jody said. At least she hadn't used her spear.

Chael felt easier once they were in orbit. The smooth humming of the ship's engines and the endless night on their screens were a comfort to him. Far below, Shadriss was a dusty gold world laced with narrow seas. Mave sat quietly in the pilot's seat, her eyes on the controls. Chael was next to her in the co-pilot's place. He shifted his weight again, trying to ease his bruises.

Their early morning call on the ship's com-screen had produced only a bland, bureaucratic sidestep. The Regent was in conference and couldn't be reached. Would they care to leave a message? Mave had decided to stick to the original plan.

"I wish we could head out right now," said Chael. "I'd like to forget about waiting for the Regent."

There was a soft movement behind them.

"You shall have your wish, outlander."

Startled, he turned. He heard Mave gasp.

"Lissa!" he cried.

"What are you doing here?" Mave demanded.

"I'm commandeering your ship," she said.

"But how—You were in the med-center!" Chael exclaimed.

"She didn't tell you?" She glanced at the chief trader. "No. I see she did not. I left the med-center some time ago. Surely, they informed t'Verra."

"Only yesterday," Mave said. She turned to Chael. "There wasn't time to tell you."

"It doesn't matter," the renegade trader said. "I want you to set course for Ozine Station. We will leave at once."

"We can't," Mave protested. "We'll run right into the Dann, and the Regent isn't ready yet."

"Exactly. With any luck, Prince Graff will decide not to risk his fleet. He's known to prefer a sure victory."

"You sound as though you want the Dann to have Ozine Station," said Chael.

She laughed, a delicate chiming peal, but her blue eyes were cold.

"Haven't you guessed?" she asked, sounding amused. "I am Dann." She bowed slightly, mockingly. "Sullat, commander of the Dann." She glanced slyly at Mave. "And in your Household."

Chael felt astonishment, grief, and the beginnings of understanding. Beside him, Mave trembled with anger.

"I don't believe you," the chief trader said. "You're lying."

"Believe what you please," Sullat told her. "It was easy enough to fool you." She looked at Chael. "The outlander knows."

Chael nodded. "You killed her, didn't you? You burned her down as she ran through the door."

"Of course," Sullat agreed, brushing her pale blonde hair away from her eyes. "We're masters of chromosonal surgery—even the League admits that—and I'm a perfect duplicate, but it would have been awkward to have the real t'Verra Lissa return to the Station. You nearly spoiled everything when you blundered in talking about a dead stranger with blonde hair. At least you brought back my wand after that fool grabbed it and tried to run."

"But why?" Mave asked, forced to believe at last. "Why have you done this?"

"To take the Station, of course. You were right all along we shall use Ozine technology to defeat the League. In the form of one of your people, it was easy

163

for me to hide a cache of weapons, even easier to lead the attack when Henyab offered to parley, as I ordered.''

"Oh, yes," she said angrily, turning on Chael. "It all worked well until you dragged me off to that filthy ball of ice. And that girl there—I'll see to her yet. She hurt me, but afterwards it seemed only sensible to ride in comfort on the sledge."

"It was you I almost caught on the Tigris, wasn't it?" Chael demanded.

"Yes, and given another minute, you would have been dead."

She glared at him, and he wondered how he ever could have felt anything for her. Mave had heard enough. She was out of the seat and on Sullat before Chael could move. The Dann seemed to blur. There was a flicker of motion, and Mave was on the floor, clutching a broken arm.

"That was foolish," said Sullat. "I can move at least five times faster than either of you. Now get up trader, and set course for Ozine Station."

Mave looked ready to defy her.

"I don't need the outlander," Sullat told her.

Reluctantly, Mave turned to the controls.

15

The trip lasted twelve standard hours. Sullat watched them constantly. She never seemed to relax. But Chael noticed that after her brief bout with Mave, she went to the emergency rations and chewed greedily on one of the tasteless chunks. Maybe that superhuman speed wasn't matched by superhuman endurance. Maybe, he thought, a few seconds at that speed tired her as much as several minutes of ordinary effort. It would be a dangerous theory to test, but it might yet come to that, he thought as he set Mave's broken arm.

It was a relief when the approach buzzer finally went off. They dropped out of hyper a scant twenty diameters from Ozine Station. Too close maybe, but there was no star and no nearby planets to worry about. The com-unit demanded their identification, and Sullat switched it on, keeping a wary eye on them as she did so.

"This is Sullat," she snapped, as Henyab's face appeared. "Bring us down on a tractor beam. I've got the chief trader and the outlander with me." It was plain that she was taking no chance on any last-minute heroics.

"Right away," Henyab said.

Almost immediately, the beam began pulling them to the surface. Their descent was slow, and Chael had several long minutes to worry about the future. He glanced at Mave. She smiled back bravely enough, but she knew their chances as well as he did. They'd be dead just as soon as Sullat had no further use for them.

They landed with a gentle thump as the tractor beam relased the War Hound just millimeters above the surface. Sullat brought out three of the Ozine belts.

"Don't try anything," she warned.

Soon, they were enveloped in the silvery haze of the suits. Chael limped heavily, exaggerating the stiffness he felt. The weaker Sullat believed them to be, the less closely she'd guard them, or so he hoped. They cycled through the airlock and emerged in the main hall. He smelled sweat, musky bodies, cooking smells, and the all-prevasive spicy oder of stim. The Dann had set up their headquarters in the main hallway. Henyab came towards them.

"Is everything under control?" Sullat asked.

"All except for a group of Ozine that are hiding in the lower levels," Henyab said.

"They'll be no threat." Sullat pointed to Chael and Mave. "Put these two with the others. It will give us two more subjects when we're ready to begin the stim experiments." She didn't look at them again.

They were led away with two guards apiece; no chance to try to escape, even if Mave weren't injured. After a long discouraging tramp, they passed the familiar red line that marked the entrance to the traders' territory. Now it was their cage. Just beyond the line, the skin-prickling buzz of a force screen blocked the corridor. The lead guard hit the release button on the grey control box on the floor in front of the screen, and the hum died.

"Inside," he ordered.

They crossed over into their prison, and the screen went up behind them. Chael followed Mave into the trader's common room.

"Cowards!" Ona cried furiously. "You don't deserve to live. I refuse to mate with such mewling fools."

She held her spear ready. Jody drew his blaster. He didn't see how they were going to get out of this without bloodshed.

"But you must lead the Station," Katt told her. "We have forseen the arrival of the Regenetrix. She will lead us to new life."

"If I'm your chief, you'll do what I say, not the other way around," Ona said. "And I say forget about this stupid breeding and fight the Dann."

166

"Mave!" Sandar exclaimed as they entered. The surviving Household rushed to embrace her, heedless of the plasticast on her arm.

"But you're trapped, too," he said. He had one arm in a crude sling. Their joy at seeing Mave was marred by fear. "You shouldn't have come back."

"I didn't intend to arrive in precisely this way, Sandar," she said, touching his arm. "We've been betrayed." And she told them about the role Sullat had played.

"She killed the real Lissa?" Sandar asked, appalled.

"Shortly after she arrived," Mave affirmed. "Sullat came here via the wand and took her place."

Chael was amazed at the change in them. At first, the Household had seemed dismayed, without direction, but now they had a focus for their anger, and they had Mave.

"League troops and the trader fleet are on their way," she said confidently, "but with the Dann controlling the landing field, all they can do is blast the Station from space, and no one wants to destroy Ozine Station."

"But what can we do?" Sandar asked, speaking for them all. "We've already tried to break out. It just threw away three more lives."

Chael wasn't listening. He stared up at the curving ceiling, feeling the cool breeze blow against his grimy face. Perhaps the traders were so familiar with their quarters that they'd overlooked the obvious.

"There's got to be an opening up there somewhere," he said. "If we can find the ventilation grill . . . ." His voice trailed off. The ceiling appeared to be an unbroken expanse of ivory, but he felt the fresh breeze. It had to be coming from somewhere above. He stepped back to where the breeze seemed strongest. The traders watched him intently.

167

"Lift me up," he called. "I think I've found it."

Hands grabbed his legs and raised him nearer the ivory dome. Still, he saw no break in the smooth plastic, but the breeze felt stronger then ever. It would be ironic if they were defeated by some form of Ozine technology now, he thought, as he searched for an opening with his fingertips. But not even the Ozine could move air through solid rock. There! He felt the strong current of cool air emerging, feeling almost like water. But the plastic was unbroken.

"I've found it," he called. "Give me something to break through with."

Someone handed him a length of metal ripped from a piece of furniture. He braced himself as best he could against the shoulders of the men supporting him, then thrust where he judged the vent to be. The end of the bar thudded against the plastic and slid aside, but the grill showed a crack across its length. A few more blows sent the rest of it raining to the floor. Above him, Chael saw a vent hole about a meter square that opened into a shaft big enough for them to walk upright. It took only a few minutes to construct a makeshift ladder.

Chael counted a dozen traders as the Household swarmed up the ladder. With Mave and himself, that still made a very small force to pit against the Dann. But they'd taken the first step, he thought as he hoisted himself into the shaft. With a little luck, they just might make it.

He followed the line of silhouetted figures, led by the dim glow of the light cube carried in the lead. They made their way through what seemed like interminable darkness. There was no change in the walls to guide him as they wound through the shaft, and he was soon lost. He could only trust that Mave knew what she was doing.

A long time later, the line halted. Chael wiped the grime off his face with his sleeve. Avrill's orange suit was a dirty rag. He longed for a drink of water. The air vents were sterile, but their passing had stirred the powdery grit deposited on the floors.

The woman just ahead touched his shoulder.

"Up front," she said softly.

Carefully, he squeezed past the others. Mave waited for him at the head of the line. She stood next to another large, opaque grill that blocked the tunnel.

"End of the line," she said. "Unless we can get through here."

"Where are we?" he asked.

"Maintenance level, well below the living quarters."

"No Dann?"

She shrugged. "Probably not." By the light of the cube, she looked pale and strained.

"All right. Stand back."

He raised the bar. He'd brought it along as a weapon, but it could serve as a tool once more. He swung, and the bar bounced back. The plastic grill shivered but held firm. Methodically, he attacked it again, and that same machine-like persistence that had served him well in the past took over. Sweat poured down his back, and his hand stung, but at last the grill gave way. Chael faced a large open area full of quietly humming machinery. The bottom of the shaft was only a step above the floor. He jumped down, and Mave followed. The net fell on them without warning.

"Run!" Chael yelled, struggling with the tightening coils, but the traders poured out of the shaft, ready for battle. Twisting, Chael fell on his back and stared up at the oddly primitive spear held at his throat, then past the spear to the golden eyes and dark hair of the Wolf-witch.

169

"Stop!" he shouted, recognizing her. "They're friends. Stop the fighting."

Slowly, the combatants turned to stare at him."

"We came in a two-man scout," Jody explained after they'd been extricated from the net. "It's hidden in a crater."

"But where is our fleet?" asked Mave.

"On its way," he replied. "Ona wanted to see what we could stir up on our own."

And what Ona wanted, Ona got, Chael added silently. Jody's knowledge of the unwarlike nature of the Ozine of Ozine Station wouldn't matter to her.

"These fools are afraid to fight, even for their home," Ona spat. "They claim I'm their chief, but they're afraid to follow my orders."

"The Ozine do not kill," said a familiar voice. "Not even at the command of the Regenetrix."

"Katt!" Chael exclaimed. "And Sinshee," he added, catching sight of his Ozine friend. He turned back to Katt. "But what do you mean, Regenetrix?"

"Just what I've always meant," Katt replied, going off on a typically Ozine tangent. "The Regenetrix has arrived to take command of Ozine Station, just as we have predicted for generations."

"But they won't fight!" wailed the Regenetrix, brandishing her spear.

"They set that net trap neatly enough," Sandar observed.

"Yes, but only after they were sure it wouldn't hurt anyone. If we'd caught any Dann, they'd have just watched while I fought them all by myself."

"Not quite by yourself," Jody put in.

Chael noted the blaster on his hip, and was glad he'd had to face only Ona with her spear.

"You have us to help you now," Mave said. The others nodded.

"We will not take part in any killing," Katt insisted. "It is not our way."

"It shall become your way," Ona hissed. "I order it so. You will obey me or die yourself." She ended with the point of her spear against Katt's throat.

"Wait!" Chael said. "This isn't necessary."

He turned to look over the assembled Ozine. There were perhaps fifty of them, in addition to Katt, Sinshee, and Ona. It was obvious to him now that they'd expected Ona to act the glorified breeder of their dying race, but they'd gotten more than they expected when they decided to take on the Wolf-witch. He'd worry about the implications of that later.

"Katt, can you help us if it doesn't involve killing anyone?"

"I suppose so," the Ozine Leader answered.

"Could you drop the net again?"

"Yes, but—"

"Good," Chael said, turning to the others. He had the glimmerings of a plan. Now, if he could just get this stubborn, opinionated non-army to work together . . . .

Chael peered cautiously over the edge of the catwalk, but no one below noticed him. The Dann were scattered in clusters on the vast cavern floor. As nearly as he could estimate, there were some three hundred invaders spread below them, and undoubtedly more in the other tunnels. He crawled back to where the others crouched.

"We've got to get them all together," he said. "We don't have time or firepower to pick them off one at a time."

"But how?" Jody asked.

Chael considered. What they needed was a loud spectacular distraction that would send the Dann scurrying to get it under control. He surveyed the dome, looking for something to aid them. His attention was caught by the light strips that crossed the ceiling. From the catwalk they were on, they had access to the maintenance center for the strips. With the right tools and a little rewiring, they ought to have a most satisfactory distraction.

The tools were there, but the job was far from simple. Chael sweated over the solid-state circuitry, carefully redrawing the pathways of power with an electromagnetic graver. There was one final cube to redraw. His hands shook, and his vision blurred as he forced himself to follow the readout on the graver's data screen.

Sandar entered. "Something's up. They're buzzing as if something big's come up."

"Maybe they've discovered we're missing," Mave said.

"It could be the fleet," Jody put in.

No one added anything to that. Chael felt the pressure on him double. They had to free the landing field at once, or the Dann would sit safely behind the surface guns and destroy the traders while they hung suspended in space. Sweat trickled past his eyes, and Mave wiped it away for him. He forced himself to concentrate; to still his hands, breathe evenly, and finish the delicate task. Finally, the last line was drawn. He let out a shaky breath and slipped the cube in place. The others watched tensely.

Chael flipped the power on full, and a smooth hum filled the room as the regular generators took over from the auxiliaries. But within moments, the sound took on a basso throb. The light strips above the dome flickered randomly—all except for one strip, near the far end of the oval. Here, the redrawn lines aimed all the power intended for the vast dome. The strip glowed searing white. Lightning crackled from it. Confusion and choas spread among the Dann.

"Come on," Chael yelled. "Head for the control room."

Quickly, the others followed him. Shadows and blue-white light flickered alternately, leaving them nearly blinded. But they were in better control than the Dann. The first Dann unfortunate enough to blunder into their squad went down with Ona's spear in his throat, and Jody blasted the second.

Chael collected their blasters and handed one to Mave. Both were on full charge. More Dann died in the access corridor leading to the control room. Each of the traders had a weapon of some sort and made good use of it.

They hit the archway opening into the control room at a dead run, silent until Ona gave vent to the yodeling scream of the Wolf people. Blaster bolts burned by. Fire and lightning arced from the wall near him. Chael rolled forward under a rain of molten metal that seared his hand and face. His feet hit the floor, and he shot a Dann. The raider folded, clawed hands clutching a gaping hole in his midsection.

A club whistled by his head. Chael ducked, but the blow landed on his shoulder, sending a line of nausea and pain through him. His blaster dropped from numb fingers as he reeled back. Helpless, he watched the club rise for a killing strike. The Dann had blue feathers, he noticed, irridescent, like oil on water. The club poised above him, suspended. Then he saw the growing streak of scarlet in the blue chest. Slowly, the Dann dropped to his knees, the club bouncing at Chael's feet. Ona pulled her spear out of the Dann's back and tossed a blaster to Chael. He caught it left-handed. The barbarian Ozine whirled and left him.

A blaster bolt sizzled by his head. Chael fired with

his metal hand and missed. He was out of practice. The Dann shot at him again, then went down under fire from one of the traders.

Chael spotted Jody locked in combat with a Dann raider twice his size. The young trader had lost his blaster, and the huge Dann lunged for him. Jody kicked savagely, and his hand chopped like an axe at the raider's neck. The Dann shook his head and kept coming. One hand closed around Jody's throat. Chael shot the Dann in the head.

"Thanks," Jody said, gasping for breath. He stooped and retrieved his blaster.

The control room was chaos. Dann and trader dead lay twisted grotesquely on the bloody floor. The reek of ions and the smoke of burned flesh sickened him. He counted the bodies as best he could through the haze and confusion. They'd lost nearly a third of the traders, and the Ozine were nowhere in sight. The Dann showed no sign of weakening. Just then, the huge monitor screen lighted up, showing golden sparks emerging into norm-space.

"The fleet!" Jody yelled.

The battle took on a new fury. Every second counted now. On the screen, laser cannon slashed the infinite night, and shields flared purple. The trader squad was too small to take the control room, but they hindered the Dann counterattack. The golden ships won to the surface one by one. The battered traders were replaced by fresh fighters. The Dann fought furiously—until a second set of lights signaled the arrival of the League ships from Shadriss. The Dann broke and ran. The traders chased them down the corridor. Chael ran after the rest, fury driving the pain from his body.

Then he saw Sullat just ahead of him. She ran easily, with confidence. Turning quickly, she ducked down a side corridor. Chael followed her. It was a narrow little-used way. The sounds of the battle were soon muted. Chael kept well back, and Sullat didn't look behind her. Then, suddenly, the corridor opened into a large room. Sullat rushed to the table at the far end and picked up the device that lay there—the wand, the doorway to anywhere. Turning, she saw Chael at last. Their eyes locked for a long moment. He reminded himself that this was the Dann leader, Sullat, but he didn't believe it. He ought to kill her. He couldn't move.

Slowly, she smiled. "Come with me, Chael," she said, and her voice was Lissa's voice. "There's no place for you here." She searched his face. "I need you."

Chael stood frozen. He wanted her, and he hated her. His finger trembled on the trigger of the blaster. She stepped closer, her arms outstretched.

Chael spun as he heard a soft step behind him. Mave paused, framed in the doorway. Snarling, Sullat rushed past him, her beautiful stolen face contorted with hate. Her blaster spat once, before Chael could act. He saw Mave fall. Then he dove for the Dann.

Fire crackeled past his ear, but he grabbed the blaster with his metal hand. Sullat was a blur. She screamed and swore at him in a language he didn't understand. Grimmly, Chael held on. Incredibly swift, she twisted, kicking savagely. Chael felt the blaster barrel bend. Sullat seemed to weaken, to slow. He could see her face now, and it was haggard. Abruptly, she let go and left him holding the ruined weapon. Chael threw it away and dove for Mave's dropped blaster.

Sullat bent over the chief trader, intent on her enemy. Chael's finger clenched, and Sullat danced backward as the beam hit her. Her body slammed convulsively against the wall and slid slowly to the floor. The fabulous Ozine wand was a mass of smoking plastic. Chael bent over Mave. She was still breathing—barely.

EPILOGUE

The War Hound crouched impatiently on the landing field. Chael felt the ache in his own bones to be off. The time for farewells was past.

"Remember," Mave said, "you have a place in my Household whenever you want it."

Her hand was on his arm. The chief trader was free now, her long bondage ended. The barbarian Wolf-witch led the Ozine, and under Ona's rule, the Station could defend itself. The Regent had returned reluctantly to Shadriss and the traders to their trading. For himself, he had business elsewhere.

He smiled and hugged Mave gently. She was still thin and pale from her recent bout with death. Sullat had failed in her murderous task by only the merest fraction.

"I'll remember," he promised, releasing her. Someday, maybe, he'd return and accept her offer, but not now, not yet.

"Don't forget us," Jody commanded, his arm around Chael's shoulders.

"Come back soon," they all said.

Then the last toasts were drunk, the last bottle emptied. Chael embraced them all once again and climbed aboard the War Hound, Mave's gift to him. He punched in the course. He was bound for the Rim—for freedom.